CHAPTER ONE

PENINA ROSS

Ugh, here he comes.

I ducked my head and nearly stared a hole through the wood grain of the bar, praying I'd gotten it wrong and that Rich Durbin, my ex-boyfriend, was not approaching me and we hadn't locked eyes a few seconds ago. *What did my gaze reveal?* I was sure I hadn't shown more than how shocked I was to see him in Bellies Bar and Grill. According to the great Rich Durbin, backup quarterback for the New Orleans Quest, the eatery, which catered mostly to those who worked at Unity Memorial Hospital across the street, wasn't cool enough for him. The spots he frequented always had plenty of professional athletes with their entourages and groupies.

I squeezed my eyes shut to think. In a matter of seconds, I would know if Rich was coming to see me or not. We'd broken up at the end of summer, which meant I hadn't seen him for two, nearly three months. *Have I missed him? Perhaps a smidgen, maybe not.* I'd been so busy at the hospital that time without him flew by. However, we had dated for three years, which was one thousand ninety-four days too long.

Rich was a serial cheater and, like most men, wasn't that good at it. I used to occasionally receive phone calls from random women informing me that my boyfriend had given her an STD, which was never transmitted to me. I never slept with him without a condom. Instinct always warned me to protect myself in that department, and I always followed my gut.

Also, the occasional girl came into the hospital, requesting me as their physician, only to learn that I was a neurosurgery resident, which meant that if her brain didn't need to be sliced open for any reason, and bad judgment for getting involved with Rich didn't qualify, then I was the wrong doctor for her.

Sometimes the crazies showed up where I lived and banged on my door. After the fourth time that happened, I developed a process with Jamie, the building manager. I would call her. She would call her brother Joe, who was a local police officer, and he and his partner would stop by and escort the crazy lady out of the building and threaten to arrest her for trespassing if she showed up again.

To say that dating Rich Durbin had been stressful was an understatement. It would be a spring day in hell before I went back to him.

However, when a large hand came down on my back, I knew I couldn't escape him.

"Pen," he said jollily, as if he was ultra-excited to see me.

Everyone called me Pen, short for Penina. I hated my name. Grade school bullies had had a field day with it. I'd been called Pinhead, Pin the Tail on the Donkey, and other silly insults that were only funny to fifth graders.

I smiled hesitantly. "Rich? What are you doing here?"

He freely put his arm around my upper back and guided me in for a hug. "You look good, as usual."

I squeezed my arms against the sides of my chest, remembering how I never wanted him to touch me again. He had also avoided answering a direct question. Experience had taught me that he was hiding something, and such secrets usually involved another woman. Suddenly, all I wanted him to do was get as far away from me as possible. The feeling was like being overtaken by a wave of severe PMS. I wanted him to evaporate into thin air and get out of my life forever.

Rich pointed at the glass in front of me. "Wait, you're drinking alcohol?"

"It's tonic water with lemon," I mumbled and pointed at my wings. "I'm here for a bite before heading home, but you already know that."

He sneered. "To sleep, then you're back at the hospital to do it again and again and fucking again."

My brow furrowed. "Yeah," I said, remembering how he'd complained about the exorbitant amount of time I spent at the hospital. "So, why are you here again?"

He sniffed then scratched an eyebrow before donning his famous lopsided smile. The expression used to give me butterflies but not anymore. It was official. I was over him.

"I'm here because I'm meeting someone," he said.

Even though I was tired after an on-call shift and didn't feel like carrying on a conversation, I piped up, "Oh, are you meeting one of the ortho surgeons?"

My question wasn't out of the realm of possibility. I'd met Rich because on the day Dr. Nordoff was to perform an arthroscopic surgery to repair his wrist, Rich passed out in the bed. His CT scan revealed a brain bleed. If he hadn't been in the hospital already, he could've died. I was the resident assigned to him. During my post-surgery rounds, the first question I asked him was "How are you feeling today, Mr. Durbin?"

He went from appearing irritated about being bedridden to flashing his charming smile. "Better now that you're here..." His eyebrows rose as he studied my name tag. "Whoa, the beautiful Dr. Ross. Today's my lucky day."

I was used to being hit on by male patients, but I would never cross that line. My patients needed to view me as a medical professional only, especially when their health and, oftentimes, their lives, depended on me. Plus, a relationship was the last thing I had room for in my life, so initially, I kept our interactions genial but professional. However, every time I walked into his hospital room, Rich's face would light up. He would engage me in conversation, which always ended up with me revealing something to him I hadn't known about myself. My revelations weren't deep, but they were certainly delightful. For instance, I didn't know I loved The Southern Candymakers so much until I told him how often I walked down to their store on Decatur to buy turtles and pralines to help get me through a night-call shift. Or whenever I had a few moments to spare, I liked to visit old cemeteries just to remind myself how old the city was. He seemed so delighted by everything I said. For a professional athlete, I found him down to earth and nice back then, cute too with his wavy neck-length brown hair and seductive brown eyes. Rich also had a powerful frame, the sort that would have made him a champion gladiator.

On the day he checked out of the hospital, he held my hand for way too long and said, "I'm not over you yet, Dr. Ross."

I just smiled, feeling no need to tell him that I hadn't felt the same way.

Then the next day, he sent enough turtles and pralines from The Southern Candymakers to make the day of our entire ward. It went on for a week, and each delivery came with a card that had a message that said something like, "Beauty and brains, my perfect woman" or, "Practice went perfect because of your healing hands, Dr. Beautiful."

One day, he personally delivered the candy himself and asked me on a date in front of everyone who was at the care station. Red-faced from embarrassment and utterly charmed into submission, I said yes. One dinner led to the next, then another, and soon we were making love and referring to each other as boyfriend and girlfriend.

The more dates we went on, the more I realized we had hardly anything in common. That wasn't a bad thing—we were just different. Whenever we were together, I would smile and try to stay awake as he talked about his coach, the team, and the trainers. He had a dog named Buddy that I liked, but Buddy wasn't the reason I stayed with his owner for way past our relationship expiration date. Rich had the family I always dreamed of, headed by his father, Ray, and stepmother, Caroline, who lived in Houston, Texas. On rare occasions when he or I had precious holiday time off, Rich would fly us to Houston so that we could spend that day with his family. My favorite gatherings with the Durbins had been the Super Duper Fourth of July Texas Barbecue Cookout and the Labor Day Luncheon. The previous year, they'd hosted a mean Thanksgiving and Christmas as well. No one could do family like the Durbins. They were good at it. They were respectful of each other, and the gatherings had lots of laughing, dancing, food, and love. *Oh, the food.* The day I broke up with Rich, I knew I would miss Ray and Caroline. They would never have me without him. But the trade-off, his cheating for their company, was far more than any self-respecting woman could tolerate.

Rich still hadn't answered my question, and I was about to ask it again when he rubbed his hands together and said, "Here she comes."

I swiveled to see what had captured his attention. He was watching Courtney Peters, a nurse who worked at the hospital. Her silk camisole blouse showed off her plump, fake tits. Her long, slender legs were wrapped in tight skinny jeans, and her enormous amount of blond hair made her tiny face look even smaller. She certainly wasn't coming on or going off shift. And she was beaming at Rich as if he were her sun. I felt my heart sink into my stomach. *No way.* Courtney and I were friends, not the best of friends, but we were at least solid acquaintances. I had complained to her about Rich on several occasions. She knew what sort of dump he was. Surely, she hadn't gotten herself involved with him.

I got my answer when they greeted each other and hugged and kissed in front of me. I swallowed the lump in my throat and worked like crazy to keep my jaw from dropping.

Courtney's eyes sparkled, and a grin stretched

wide across her face when she said, "Pen, you're still around."

Speechless, I raised my hand at Roy, the bartender, to let him know I was ready to pay for my wings. "Not anymore," I muttered, feeling ambushed.

Roy slid a basket of wings and fries in front of another patron. "Can I put it on your tab? I'm busy."

I nodded. Bellies was almost always packed at that hour. I heard they had the best drinks in the vicinity. They certainly had the best bourbon wings. I swiped my bag off the back of my stool, ready to escape the presence of my ex and the chipper and backstabbing nurse as fast as I could.

"No, stay. Have a drink with us," Courtney said. She was smiling as if the picture she was presenting by standing next to my ex with his arm around her was acceptable.

My gaze flitted between the two of them, then I slid out of my seat. "Sorry, I've been here too long already." My smile couldn't be faker as I said, "But you guys enjoy yourselves."

Courtney stepped in front of me to block my path. Her brazenness made me draw back and assess the situation further. Not only was she in my way, but she had something purposeful about her expression. I felt it was by no accident she and Rich were standing in front of me.

"So, I invited you to my Midsummer's Night NOLA-Style Feast, remember?" Courtney sang as if she was about to break some bad news to me.

I tipped my head back and said, "Yeah."

Courtney was hosting the most popular party of the year. Everyone in our ward was invited, and I was counting on being there. I hated being left out. Not only that, but I wasn't a fan of being alone for too long either. I had no family that hosted big gatherings or lavish parties. I hardly had any family at all. My mother was missing in action yet again, and I'd never met my father. My aunt Christine, my mother's sister, was in my life, but we rarely visited each other.

Courtney touched my hand as if she were consoling me, and perhaps she was. The look on my face probably made her think she needed to. "I… we…" She rubbed Rich's massive back. "Just wanted to let you know that we're a couple before you show up at the party, and well… you know." She turned the corners of her mouth down as if she could feel the severe heartache I was supposed to be experiencing.

I wasn't a snide person, but I fought the urge to

behave as one and say something like, *No, Court, I don't know, and may his perpetually itchy dick give you itchy pussy.*

Instead I forced a smile. "Sure," I said in a strained voice and cleared my throat. "And really, I don't have a problem with the two of you being together. Um, congratulations."

I hoped that was the truth and felt that it was, sort of. I didn't want to be disinvited from the biggest party of the year. Everyone was going. Dr. Deb Glasgow, our chief resident, had created a killer schedule designed to make sure everyone worked a limited number of hours on the day before, of, and after the party so that we could eat, drink, dance, and stay out as long as our hearts desired. I would be working three hours on night call, which meant I would be as fresh as a baby's powdered bottom, which wasn't my usual state. The rest of my colleagues and I were perpetually exhausted and would be so until the last day of our residency. I had a month and a half to go.

"Great," Courtney sang. I could tell she either didn't believe me or didn't want to. She was the sort of girl who acquired a morsel of gratification from having something someone else coveted. That was because she liked to show off her toys—new shoes, new jewelry, new purse, new boyfriend, big new house, new this or that—and would simper as she watched everyone say ooh and ahh.

"Well, okay, then. Goodbye," I said in a rush, wanting to vacate the scene at warp speed.

"Are you sure you don't want to stay and have a drink?" Courtney asked.

"She doesn't drink," Rich said.

I narrowed my eyes at him then fake-smiled at Courtney again. His purporting to know what I did or didn't do bothered me. He wasn't my boyfriend, which meant he was no longer allowed to talk about my habits. That was such an intimate thing to do.

Thumbing toward the exit, I said, "I'm on the back end of a thirty-hour shift. So, I'm leaving."

Before I could take a step back, Courtney hugged me. She always smelled like a strawberries and sweet perfume. I avoided looking at Rich, but I could feel him watching me.

"I'm glad you're cool about this," she said, still squeezing me. "I was worried. I mean, we can't help who we fall in love with, can we?"

Instead of shouting, "Bullshit," I gave another tight smile then said, "Right, uh-huh. Goodbye," before walking away as fast as I could, maneuvering past tables like a pinball, on my way out of Bellies.

The nearby Mississippi River made the humidity more intense. I wasn't one of those people who was made famished by too much humidity, though. I was from the dry desert, and the New Orleans air reminded me how far away I was from my early days. After the excitement from my encounter with Rich and Court, I remembered how exhausted I was, but I'd been drained since day one of my residency, so it wasn't that much of a distraction. With each step, I couldn't shake out of my head the picture of the two of them standing beside each other, appearing as though they were the perfect couple. I didn't feel the least bit sorry for Courtney, though. She had been forewarned about Rich. If she wanted to date a serial cheater, then she would get what she signed up for.

As I plodded along, my legs and arms were as heavy as cinder blocks, and the dull ache in my head warned me that my grace period to be awake was almost over. I usually slept well once I crawled into bed and put my eye mask on. However, I was beginning to fear that what happened at Bellies might continue to vex me and, as a result, disturb my precious sleep. Suddenly, my mental image of them morphed into a plastic couple on top of a wedding cake. Soon, she would be able to hobnob with Caroline and Ray. I had no doubt they would like Courtney. She could hoot it up with the best of them, even if her cheery, dearie, fun-girl-slash-good-girl persona was fake.

I forced myself to pay attention to cute shops I passed as I walked under wraparound balconies. I worked and lived in the Warehouse District. Each day, I was reminded of why I'd chosen to do my residency in New Orleans. I'd become enamored with the city during my freshman year of college. Nat, my then-dormmate, was from Baton Rouge. Every Thanksgiving, I would go home with her for the holiday, and we would make our way to the Big Easy to party on Frenchman Street. The live bands, the excitement, the dancing, and the boys all merged to be the most exhilarating experience ever. I thought for certain the partying and fun would continue, but I hadn't been able to partake in either since day one of my residency.

Finally, my building was in sight, and I released the tension in my shoulders a bit. I lived on the third floor of a four-story apartment complex that used to be a brick warehouse. Feeling as if I were almost on my last leg, I stared at the iron gate that stood between me and the front door. As I repeated my gate code to myself, which was something I did to keep my eyes open, a tall drink of water walked out onto the stoop.

My brow furrowed and released as my gaze locked in on him. The more I advanced, the harder it was to look away. I'd never seen the guy before. All tenants in the building worked at the hospital in some capacity, so I'd seen just about everyone before but never him. I was drawn to his strong posture the most. Truly confident men always turned me on. I watched as he shook a cigarette out of a package, put the stick in his mouth, and lit it.

Our eyes met. At first, his glance was fleeting, but then he did a double take. I was breathless as his eyes roamed my face. My cheeks felt hot, and I nervously shifted my bag from one shoulder to the other. *Why is he watching me that way?* I waited for his gaze to release me, but the closer I got, the tighter it held me. I couldn't look away from him either.

As I closed the gap between us, his looks took my breath away. He was unusually handsome. I wasn't well versed in male celebrities since I barely had time to watch TV and couldn't remember the last time I'd seen a movie, but I was certain that if he were an actor, his pale-blue eyes and sharp features would've made him a sex symbol.

Then I finished walking up the three steps that led to the entrance.

"Hi," I said past my tight throat.

My nervousness made my fingers jerky as I punched in my code. The guy still hadn't responded, although he had finally taken his eyes off me. He took another draw on his cigarette then smashed it out on a nearby planter.

The lock buzzed. He still hadn't replied to my greeting, and I wished I could take it back.

"What an ass," I muttered as I opened the door, determined to avoid the opposite sex forever or perhaps at least until men became better at being nicer and not picking my friends to fuck.

"Hello," he said faintly just before I closed the door behind me.

CHAPTER TWO

PENINA ROSS

My apartment was cute. It had red brick walls, light hardwood floors, and an island in the kitchen with a wood block top, which would've been great for cooking if I'd had the time for it. My office was a little alcove that was adjoined to my living room. It had a view of the building right behind mine and the small courtyard between us. It also had a modern bathroom with no tub, only a shower, and my bedroom had the same view the alcove had. The common area never got loud since most of us worked at the hospital and knew how precious silence was. The problem was that I rarely had time to enjoy living in my cute little abode.

The first things I did when I walked inside was

take my clothes off, shove them into the laundry basket, and get into the shower.

As the warm water trickled down my face, I squeezed the sides of my head, trying to expunge memories of my ex, his new girlfriend, and the stranger from my head. *What's happening to me?* I suddenly felt as if my life was about to change in ways I never imagined. Maybe Court and Rich's relationship would work, and their success would reveal that I was the one who pushed him into cheating. I was too cold, not available and when the rubber met the road, not truly in love with him.

I turned off the water, determined to keep it together and not fall apart. The shower had given me enough energy to make a quick cup of chamomile, echinacea, and ginger root tea with lemon and honey and drink it while checking my email to see if my fellowship had been approved.

As I waited for my screen to go through its motions, I thought about how bleak my life was. I lived in gray. Courtney and Rich, well, they lived in red, vibrant blue, and hot pink. That was why Rich cheated on me. He used to say it all the time. "Pen, you're sexy as hell but boring as fuck." Then he would laugh as if he were joking. I would laugh, too, because I felt boring, even though I knew I wasn't.

Work, work, work… that was all I did. I loved my job, but still, I felt trapped in a universe where it was the only thing I had going on.

When my computer booted, I went straight to my email. I'd applied for a fellowship in Boston to be closer to my aunt Christine, who lived in Cambridge, Massachusetts, and was a licensed marriage and family therapist. She wasn't the type of person who hosted family get-togethers. As a matter of fact, I'd never been to her house. When I was in medical school in Boston, we'd met for coffee or lunch occasionally, but though I wasn't that far away from her, we only met up a handful of times. The last time I'd seen her, she kept repeating how much I looked like my mom. Whenever she said it, the skin between her eyes would pucker, which made me nervous.

"If you're worried that I'm going to drop off the face of the earth like her, don't. I'm entering my residency, so…" I said, picking at my muffin on my plate.

Though I'd thought what I said would make her stop frowning, she intensified it after asking me more questions. I couldn't remember what she had asked me exactly. Perhaps it was a question about my dorm life or subjects I found more interesting. I felt as if we used to struggle to keep a conversation going. Then after one hour on the dot, Christine announced that she had to leave for one reason or another, and that would be the end of our visit.

Those sit-downs with her felt as though they had happened many moons ago, but she and I had been in touch since. Each month, she put ten thousand dollars into my account. She said it was an inheritance from my grandparents.

"An inheritance?" I asked. "I thought they came from nothing."

"No. They didn't," Christine said in her usual cool tone.

"But why now, when they've been dead since before I was born?"

"Well, that's how it goes sometimes. These things can take forever to get resolved," she said.

I hadn't needed to touch a dime of the money. I kept it in a high-interest-yielding savings account. One day, I would use the cash to buy a house. As long as my life was the way it was, I didn't need much money. Sleep was worth more than all the money in the world.

I yawned as I scanned my new emails from top to bottom—no message from Boston Medical Center. I could finally relax until I checked again the next day.

Suddenly, it was as if exhaustion hit me like a ton of bricks. I yawned yet again and dragged myself to my bedroom, crawled into bed, and went straight to sleep.

My alarm blared, fusing with my dream of the sexy stranger. We had just kissed, and he told me that Rich was his teammate. I was heartbroken about that since I didn't want anything to do with Rich or his team and tried to yell at him to stay away from me, but my mouth couldn't work.

Finally, my eyes opened, and it no longer mattered that I couldn't speak in my dream. It was over, and I had no time to explore its meaning. The rat race called my life had officially resumed.

After raking my toothbrush across my teeth as fast as I could and dousing my face with cold water, I took a moment to study my reflection in the mirror. My skin was pallid, and darkness had settled beneath my light-brown eyes. I'd looked like that for a long time, and it wouldn't get any better for a while. Soon my residency would be over, but being a fellow or an attending was just as draining.

I turned off the faucet. It was not the time to get bogged down by thinking about my future. Plus, doom and gloom might not have been in the forecast. My next shift loomed. So I rushed into the kitchen and grabbed the Ziploc bags I'd already prepped with my favorite snacks like beet chips, raw almonds, and apple slices covered with peanut butter and stuffed them into my oversized tote bag, which already contained a toothbrush, toothpaste, mouthwash, face cleanser, a face towel, two changes of underwear, two pairs of socks, and a host of other knickknacks I'd forgotten about.

Two minutes left. I gulped down a glass of orange juice, set the glass in the sink, grabbed my bag, and rushed out the front door, barely remembering to lock it.

"Morning, Kit Kat," someone with a familiar voice called.

I stopped at the elevator and turned to see Zara Agate, one of my team members, power walking in my direction as she put on her jacket. *Shit, I forgot my jacket.* Then I remembered I had an extra one stored in my locker and relaxed. Even though it was hot outside, it was often freezing cold in the hospital.

"Morning, Reese's Pieces," I said as I jabbed the elevator button.

When we'd begun our neurosurgery residency together, we spent most of our shift hungry and scarfing down packaged and chemical-laden junk food. We started calling each other by the names of our favorite snacks to make not eating any of it easier. Seven years later, we no longer craved the junk. It probably had nothing to do with the nick-names. We'd both learned that if we wanted to pull off a thirty-hour shift, which entailed at least three surgeries, then we'd better be powered by more nutritious food.

She stopped beside me and rubbed her eyes. "Another day, another shitty day."

I cracked an empathetic smile.

"And tonight, I'm on call. Shit," she groused.

The doors slid open. Calvin and Sanjay, two residents in the internal medicine program, were already inside.

"Good morning, guys," I said as Zara grabbed me by the shoulders.

"Seriously, Pen. I don't know if I'm coming or going." She was shaking me as she worked herself into a frenzy. "What am I doing with my life? Why am I so dog-tired?"

The doors opened, and Sanjay and Calvin raised their eyebrows and said, “See you later,” as they slid past us and out of the elevator. They were used to meltdowns. We all were.

I quickly took her by her shoulders and looked her dead in the eyes. “Done?”

Her frown said she was unsure. “I guess so.”

That was good enough for me. “Then let’s walk.”

I exited the elevator, and she followed me.

The NOLA air always made the new day easier for me. It was going to be another hot one, when all the fried foods and local cuisines would be simmering in the atmosphere. However, once again, I would be trapped inside the big, cold hospital, unable to catch a whiff of any of it until my shift ended.

Zara and I walked swiftly out of habit but in silence, which was abnormal. She was usually a chatterbox in the morning. It felt so strange not to hear her prattle on about her political volunteerism or the newest guy her parents were trying to get her to marry that I asked if everything was okay.

She sighed wearily. “No.”

“No?” My tone was both sympathetic and leading her to explain.

"Remember what we talked about a few days ago?"

I shuffled through my memory bank to find the last conversation we had. When I located it, I gasped a little. "You mean quitting the program. You weren't serious about that." At least I wanted to think so.

"Yeah," she said with a sigh. "I think I've had enough, Pen."

I shook my head repeatedly. "We're almost finished, though."

"No," she said and slapped herself on the chest. "*I'm* done. And I don't give a fuck if my parents are disappointed. I'm thirty-two and only became a doctor because it was either be a doctor"—she raised her finger emphatically—"no, be more than a doctor. Be a brain surgeon or marry one of their rich friends' sons. No. No, no, no, and no. I'm over it. And quitting at this point sends the strongest message to my parents that they don't control me anymore. Fuck it. If I lose them, then I lose them, but I'll be free."

We were thoughtfully silent again as we passed Bernard's Bakery. Usually, one of us would ask if the other wanted to go in for a croissant, knowing we'd be a little late for our shift because Eloise, the woman who co-owned the bakery and worked in the mornings, would want to gossip about something someone from the hospital had told her.

Actually, it would've been perfect to chat with Eloise that morning. She might've known something about the handsome stranger. My mind was too busy to obsess over him, but I still wanted to know who he was. The decadent smell of freshly baked pastries drew everyone in the neighborhood into her shop. If he lived in the area, Eloise would know his whole story. I was sure of it.

I looked longingly through the window of Bernard's. That day, we would pass her by, and that felt like the right decision.

After a sigh, I said, "Well... you are right about your life belonging to you, and that's the way God made it. You know what I mean? He didn't attach your mom and dad to your ass. You know?"

Zara pressed her lips together as she nodded. "Right," she said quietly. "By the way, what's going on with you since we last spoke?"

It almost felt wrong to bring up my dramas. That odd sense that radical change was in the air had grabbed me again, though. I certainly had a lot of newness in my life as of the day before at Bellies, but Zara wasn't just frivolously claiming she was quitting. She meant it. Half of me wanted to convince her to stay. The other half knew she couldn't be persuaded.

"Hurry, tell me. We're almost at the hospital," she said.

When I looked up from the pavement, I saw the huge modern glass complex on the horizon. So I scoffed then quickly told her about my encounter with Court and Rich.

She frowned as she shook her head slowly. "Wait, are you seriously talking about Rich Durbin, your ex?"

I nodded then shrugged nonchalantly. "Yeah." I turned to meet her gaze. "What?" I asked, confused.

"That's it?"

I jerked my head back. "What do you mean, 'that's it'?"

"You don't want to scratch her eyes out, pull her hair, or clip his balls off?"

I sniffed. "No." My tone made it clear that I thought that was the most ridiculous thing I'd ever heard. Other people behaved that way but not me. Acting like a petulant child when things didn't go my way wasn't how I operated.

She put an arm around my shoulders. "That's right, crazy-ass bitch is not your style."

I chuckled and put my arm around her waist. "Hey…"

"What?"

"Are you really leaving?" I couldn't help myself. I had to know for sure that our walks to the hospital, lunches and dinners in the call room or the fourth-floor terrace, note comparing during rounds, and competitions to fly solo on the best surgeries would end one month earlier.

She came to an abrupt stop. "Wait." She wrinkled her nose.

"What?" I slapped my hand over my chest. Curiosity made my heart beat faster.

"Haven't you ever wondered why Courtney sounds like a Valley girl straight out of the malls of the San Fernando Valley during the eighties when she was born and raised in New Orleans? Like, how the hell does that happen?"

I tossed my head back, and Zara and I laughed so hard that our voices echoed through the courtyard. Then I saw *him*, and my laughter came to an immediate halt. His curious and sexy pale-blue eyes flitted over Zara's face then landed on mine. I couldn't breathe, though I thought I'd just gasped. Zara and I were silent as church mice as we finished watching him stroll into the hospital.

It took a moment for the details about him to work their way through my brain. He had on a white lab coat over blue scrubs, and he looked even yummier than he had the day before.

"Who the hell was that?" she asked, her jaw still dropped.

"I don't know," I said breathlessly.

"He's into you," she said.

I shook my head adamantly. "No way. You're the beauty. I'm not."

"Oh, fuck, Pen. What's wrong with you?"

My neck jutted forward. "Huh?"

"Ugh," she grunted, frustrated. "Let's go. Hot doctor has made us extra late. And we need to learn who the hell he is so you can get laid."

I gasped, and my mouth remained open as she practically dragged me past the sliding glass doors. Deep down inside, I was scared, and I was certain that not even in an alternate universe or another lifetime would someone who carried himself and looked like that guy be into me. *Right?*

CHAPTER THREE

PENINA ROSS

His name was Dr. Jake Sparrow, and out of all the departments in the hospital, he was in mine—or better yet, since he was an attending, I was in his. I had managed to avoid directly interacting with him all day. However, whenever we were in the same room, I could sense his presence. I caught him staring at me numerous times. It was strange, though. It was as if he didn't know he was doing it. For instance, when he spoke with Dr. Nassim, one of the fellows, while he listened, he stared at me. I tried like hell to avoid his eyes and escape the room as fast as I could. *What is it about him?* I'd never had such a reaction to a man.

My shift went along as it usually did. Most people didn't like doing rounds as much as I did.

There was something about entering a room and seeing hope in their eyes that I had good news about the patient's condition. Even when I had not so good news to give them, I tried to make our encounter an optimistic one.

Along with the patients that were assigned to me the other day, I had picked up new ones after night call handed off their recently admitted patients. I read their charts and studied lab results and scans, wanting to know it all. After rounds, I was paged to the OR to perform my first endovascular repair of the day. Nearly every day, I encountered patients who bore stifling headaches until they ended up in the emergency room, barely hanging on for dear life. As a seventh-year resident, I could perform all surgical procedures without guidance. Only an attending had to sign off on the surgery. One day, Jake Sparrow and I would have to communicate, but that day wasn't then.

My shift was almost over, and as usual, it went by so fast. I was standing at the electronic health record pod in the care station while charting when Zara and Deb, our chief resident, walked out of one of the conference rooms. I stared hard at Zara, willing her to look at me. But she kept her eyes down as she walked past everyone in the vicinity then up the hallway that led to the call room.

I was about to tear away from the EMR module to catch up with Zara and question her, but Deb stomped toward me. Her lips were pressed into a flat line, and the corners of her mouth turned downward.

When she reached me, she patted the counter twice. "Could you take Zara's on-call night tonight? I'll give you two days off for it."

"Sure," I said, still troubled by the mystery of whether Zara had gone through with her plan to quit.

"Thanks," Deb said and walked away from me before I could ask what happened between the two of them. "Oh." She stopped in her tracks.

I raised my eyebrows.

"I'm putting you on Dr. Sparrow's service this evening. It'll be good for you to pick up as many techniques from him as you can while you're still here." She checked her wristwatch. "He'll be in surgery in forty-five minutes, OR seven. You should get prepped now."

It felt as if my head were rising to the ceiling. *No. I managed to avoid him all day, and now I'm going to be in surgery with him?* My terrified eyes remained pasted to Deb's back. I tried to think of something to say, but my mouth wouldn't work. I wanted to take it back and say I couldn't cover for Zara because I had a thing to attend that night and couldn't get out of it. *What thing?* I couldn't think of one.

Soon Deb was out of sight, and there was no turning back. I couldn't avoid the mysterious, sexy, and quite rude new attending.

"You okay?" John Ness, one of the oncology residents, asked.

I hadn't noticed him standing next to me and could only imagine how flustered I appeared. So I stood up straight, pulled my shoulders back, and decided to face Dr. Sparrow with confidence and professionalism.

"I'm fine."

Really, I am.

I WASN'T FINE.

I prepped for the assist on a decompressive craniectomy, which was when part of the patient's skull would be removed to relieve the pressure of swelling in the brain. I had performed two of those surgeries by myself earlier that week. The odds of a patient dying were high. According to Melanie, the OR assistant who scrubbed in with me, Dr. Sparrow was on his eighth straight surgery and would appreciate a resident of my caliber scrubbing in to make sure he didn't miss a step. He had been expecting Zara, but according to Melanie, I was the better option. Melanie and Zara had strange tension between them, so I thought it best not to comment.

"But Dr. Sparrow is top-notch," she assured me. "He's hands down the best surgeon I've had the privilege to work with."

That made me feel better about heading into a critical procedure with him. I had to bring my A game. And it sounded as if he was a consummate professional who wouldn't let the reason he'd stared at me so much get in the way of our working together. The patient's name was Bruce Landy. His motorcycle had slipped on an oil patch, which caused him to skid off the road and tumble twenty-five feet down a ravine, and his surgery would be tricky.

But as soon as I walked into the operating room, Dr. Sparrow stared at me with his mouth agape. He didn't look happy to see me. That was for sure. And I immediately felt my skin burn.

"What are you doing here?" he growled.

I couldn't believe the scorn in his tone. *What did I ever do to him but say hello?* "I'm here for an assist," I said.

"Where's Dr. Agate?"

My brow furrowed. It sort of stung that he wanted her instead of me. "She's not here, but I assure you—"

"This is not a teaching moment. You can leave," Dr. Sparrow said and looked down to verify his instruments.

Stacy, one of the nurses, stopped taping the patient's eyes to raise her eyebrows at me. I could tell she was curious about how I was going to respond.

I stood tall, planting my feet in a wide stance. "Dr. Sparrow, I assure you this is not a teaching moment. I've done this procedure on my own many times before tonight. I'm here to assist."

He looked up again and narrowed his eyes at me. *Is he staring at my mouth?* I felt something emanating from him but was sure it wasn't desire. *No way, not desire.*

Dr. Sparrow cleared his throat. "Your assistance will not be needed either. Look in on my patients instead. You can do that, can't you?" He sounded as if he was trying to talk down to me.

Stacy went back to taping the patient's eyes closed.

Since I didn't want to cry in front of him or any of the others in the room, I easily conceded. Still fully prepped for surgery, I raced down the corridor. Curious onlookers watched me. I knew I looked distressed. In all my years in the program, I had never felt so humiliated.

I stormed into the on-call room then plopped down on a bench and clutched my thighs. Dr. Sparrow was a supreme dick. Suddenly, I knew why I had been attracted to him. My picker was shit. It was as if I always fell for the one asshole in the room who was waiting to disrespect me. *Fuck him!*

"Fuck who?" someone asked.

I whipped around. I hadn't noticed Kevin Chen on the opposite side of the room, digging into his locker.

"I said that out loud?" I asked.

He nodded. "Yep."

I rolled my eyes, still steaming mad. But I was not going to complain about Sparrow and give the rude doctor the satisfaction of knowing he'd gotten to me.

"Fuck no one. I was just blowing off some steam."

"All righty then," Kevin said.

I shot to my feet. The doctor had sent me on rounds, and that was exactly what I was going to do.

I WAS AT THE BEDSIDE OF MY FOURTH PATIENT. His name was Trey Sharp, and he was thirty-seven years old and had fallen off a twenty-foot-tall scaffold while working at a construction site. He was six hours and forty-two minutes post-op on a surgery to stop a subarachnoid hemorrhage. As I read the chart, I noticed that it had been two hours since the last time his vitals were checked. I would've ordered that his vitals be checked every half hour. The hospital was going through a severe nurse shortage, which had been the case at the hospital where I attended medical school as well. It didn't take long to learn that nurse staffing was where hospitals skimped, yet their role in a patient's care program was just as vital as a surgeon's.

I was certainly capable of fulfilling the order and taking the vitals myself and was about to do it until I noticed something else. Mr. Sharp's body was extra tense, and his mouth was caught open. I checked his hands. His fists were curled up. He was seizing.

"Holy shit," I whispered.

I hit the emergency button and called for a nurse, asking for an intravenous dose of benzodiazepine. Lucy, one of the nurses, was in the room in a matter of seconds, and I administered the seizure-halting medication, which did its job immediately.

Next I called down to imaging and let them know my patient's history and told them he needed a CT scan, stat. Since an orderly wasn't immediately available to take our patient, who was groggy but finally awake, downstairs, Lucy and I rolled him to imaging.

After dropping off Mr. Sharp, I resumed my rounds but told the technician to contact me as soon as the results were ready to be looked at. I also asked that a copy be sent to Dr. Sparrow, even though he was still in surgery.

More patients were happy to see me and hear their plans of care. I was just about to forgo rushing down to the nurses' call station, where I'd heard there were an assortment of cold beignets from Bernard's Bakery, when I got the page from imaging. I was sent a code indicating that I should get downstairs fast. When I arrived at imaging and examined the results, I knew care couldn't be delayed. The guy needed to get into the OR and fast.

I contacted Deb and quickly gave her the rundown.

"But you're supposed to be scrubbed in on the craniectomy."

"He said he didn't need me and sent me on rounds."

She paused then grunted. "It's an intracerebral hemorrhage?"

"Yes," I said.

"Get Sparrow to sign off before you go into the OR."

I suppressed a gasp. "Sparrow?"

"Yes. Sparrow. Do you have a problem with him or something?"

"No," I said as relaxed as I could.

"Then I'll see you in the morning," Deb said and hung up.

I sighed forcefully as I scratched my scalp beneath my loose ponytail. Deb and I had entered the program at the same time. She opted to be chief resident. I preferred to stay where I could perform as many surgeries as possible. She was the best chief resident in the complex, but sometimes she could be an annoying hard-ass that I loved to death.

Five minutes later, I stood outside of OR seven, chewing nervously on my bottom lip, waiting for

Melanie to finish relaying my message to Dr. Sparrow about Mr. Sharp and give me the green light to save his life.

Finally, the door opened. She gave me a thumbs-up, and I immediately raced to OR three to get the surgery underway.

Six Hours Later

My shift was over, and I was ready to devour an order of bourbon wings then settle in for a long day's sleep. But first I went to check in on Mr. Sharp. When I stepped into the patient's room, he was awake but groggy from being on pain medication. Two big guys who looked the same age as the patient were standing at his bedside. I could tell they weren't meaning to stay long. They wore work boots with jeans and tan T-shirts.

I always remembered to smile when first encountering patients and their visitors. "Good morning," I said, making sure to not say it too loudly.

The men gave me funny looks, so I told them I

was Dr. Ross and I'd performed the surgery earlier that morning.

"There's no way in hell you're a surgeon," one of them said.

"Yes, sir," I said with an assured nod. I wasn't insulted by his surprise. I got that a lot. Then I focused on the patient. "Mr. Sharp, how are you doing this morning?"

He raised his thumb.

My smile broadened. "Glad to hear it. Your surgery went smoothly. Your vitals have been looking good. You're a strong man, Mr. Sharp."

"Trey. Call me Trey," he said softly.

One of his visitors extended an arm toward me. "And me, Jack."

I shook his hand.

The other guy also shot his arm out. "I'm Mike."

"Jack and Mike," I said while shaking Mike's hand.

"I don't see a ring, Doc," Mike said, still holding my hand.

"Good morning," a voice blared from behind me.

We all turned toward the doorway to see who'd spoken. It was Dr. Sparrow.

First of all, I had no idea that "good morning" was in his vocabulary since I'd never heard him say it once. The day before, while passing Zara and me on his way into the building, would've been a great time for him to say it.

As he strolled toward us with the air of a marquis, his presence filled the room. I felt dwarfed standing next to him, and I was pretty sure that was his intention.

What a dick.

Then he went on explaining to Trey's friends the procedure that I'd performed. I was supposed to do that, and I wanted to cut him off and take over.

"Well," I said as soon as Sparrow finally took a pause. "I'm going to step out. Trey, I'm glad you're feeling well this morning. The nurses will continue to check on you regularly—"

"She saved your life this morning," Sparrow said.

My body stiffened. I was shocked to hear him say that. Finally, I let my gaze meet his.

His eyebrows shifted upward and stayed there. "She did good work."

"You never answered. Are you single?" Jack asked.

I closed my mouth and swallowed as I looked at the other man. He was certainly cute but couldn't hold a candle to Dr. Sparrow. Hell, no one could hold a candle to him—not even me.

"Dude, you have a girlfriend," Mike said. "If I was over there, I'd slap you in the back of the head."

At least that got a light chuckle from Trey, who seemed to be enjoying his friends' company.

"No boyfriend," I said finally.

"Husband?" Jack fired off rapidly.

"Um..." My skin burned as I felt Sparrow watching me intently. "No. Okay..." I said in a tone indicating that I was putting an end to that line of questioning. I took a few steps away from the bed. "Nice meeting you guys, but I have to leave."

The three guys spoke their last goodbyes, and I moved out of the room fast. I heard Dr. Sparrow say something about Trey's care plan for the day. He spoke loudly, making sure those guys knew that he had the floor, and for once, I was thankful that he and I had shared the same space for a few minutes.

What was that in there, though? Why was he looking at me that way? I wondered if what I'd seen in his eyes was hate, admiration, or perhaps lust. *Nah. It couldn't have been lust. No way.*

CHAPTER FOUR

PENINA ROSS

I hadn't meant to do it, but I walked right past Bellies and headed home. I had a lot on my mind—plus, I was so exhausted that I could barely stand, let alone sit at the counter, eating chicken wings. I also wanted to preserve enough energy to confront Zara. I was shocked that she'd left without even finding me and telling me what happened. It wasn't as if I didn't know the answer. But I wanted to hear it from the horse's mouth.

She lived in the apartment next to mine. When I knocked on her door, I got no answer. I stood there for a good while, my knuckles hitting the wood.

"Looking for Zara?" someone behind me asked.

I whipped around to see Jen Lovely, an internal

medicine resident who lived in the apartment across from mine.

"Yes." I sounded desperate.

"She's gone." Her tone was casual.

I jerked my head forward. "Gone? Did she move out?"

"No," Jen said, shaking her head emphatically. "She said something about going to DC for some rally. You know how political she is and shit. Someone said she quit her residency today, though. Did she?"

Talk about someone with diarrhea of the mouth. I could neither confirm nor deny whether Zara had flushed thousands of dollars of education down the toilet, so I wasn't going to voice whether she had or not.

I shrugged. "I don't know. I haven't spoken to her."

"Isn't Deb Glasgow your chief resident?" Jen sounded anxious. Her eyes were glossy, and she had an intense look on her face. She was obviously determined to get the details before anyone else. She prided herself on knowing things first. I swore she should've been a journalist instead of a doctor.

"I haven't spoken to Deb about Zara. I was too

busy working a very long shift." I thumbed over at my door. "So, if you don't mind, I'm going to bed."

Jen took a step back. "Fine," she said, shrugging one shoulder jerkily. Then she turned her back on me, swung open the door to her apartment, went inside, and slammed the door behind her.

I rolled my eyes as I shook my head then entered my own domain. Once inside, I dropped my shit on the sofa. Then I went to the kitchen and took some Chinese takeout out of the refrigerator. It was from five or six days ago. I smelled it.

"Humph," I grunted.

It was still good, so I microwaved it.

As my food was warming, I leaned against the counter, attempting to deconstruct what had happened in the patient's room that morning. Sparrow had walked in as if he owned the world. I gathered that he was one of those boys who came from a lot of money. They were usually the most fucked up, sort of like Zara. They were only surgeons because they were fulfilling their parents' expectations. Usually, the rich boys were more artful at blowing up their careers, though. They often ended up being kicked out of the program for stealing medications, reporting to their shift high one too many times, or continuously failing tests.

But according to Melanie, Dr. Sparrow was kick-ass at his job. However, he was still a jerk.

I sniffed bitterly and muttered, "Douchebag moneybags."

But he'd said aloud that I saved Mr. Sharp's life. If he was such a bad guy, then it was weird that he would pay me a compliment like that in front of two burly men who were obviously hitting on me. Sparrow was just so damn confusing. The only way for me to stop thinking about him was to go directly to sleep.

The microwave dinged, and I took my food out of it. I grabbed a fork and scarfed down as much Kung Pao chicken as I needed to make my belly full enough to help me sleep well. Next, I stripped out of my clothes, and without showering this time since I didn't see a need to be clean while sleeping, I crawled into bed and drifted off to dreamland not long after my head hit the pillow.

I WOKE TO AN INCESSANT SOUND OF SIRENS BLARING. The more alert I became, the closer the noise felt. Then someone banged on my door, and I knew that whatever was happening was occurring in real life.

Jumping out of bed, I grabbed my cellphone. The action was automatic. The world could be ending, and a doctor knew she'd better have a means of communication on her person. Since I was naked, I jumped into an oversized T-shirt and a pair of plaid pajamas then yanked my robe off the hook on the bathroom door. Smoke was settling in the room. When I opened the front door, smoke filled the hallway.

Amy, one of the assistants who worked in the office and lived on the premises, was banging on everyone's door, screaming, "Fire! Exit the building through the stairwell!"

I could hardly believe my luck.

"Damn it," I mumbled, cursing the inconvenience. I was still as tired as hell. Whatever was happening didn't feel fair at all.

I needed shoes and to change into warmer pants, so I scuttled back inside and put on jeans and tennis shoes. I also grabbed my purse and my workbag then headed back out into the cloudy hallway.

As we padded down the stairs, I kept my hand over my mouth like the other tenants. It had been a long time since I'd seen a lot of them. We were all in distress.

We waited fifty feet away from the building,

watching the fire trucks casting their lights against the brick. A whole host of firemen had already raced inside. There was a lot of smoke but still no flames.

"What the fuck," an intern named Sarah Locke said as she stepped up beside me. "I don't see a fire. Do you see a fire?" The circles under her eyes were deep and dark, and she was shivering slightly. I recognized the sort of exhaustion she was feeling. It certainly sucked to be in her shoes. The first year as a resident was the worst year.

To console her, I put an arm around her. "You okay?" I asked.

She nodded stiffly.

"Did you just get off shift?"

Her head bobbled as she moaned, "Mm-hmm."

"This'll be over soon," I assured her. *Fingers crossed.*

Suddenly, she stood up straight as if she'd just gotten a burst of energy. "Who's that?"

I looked at her then followed her line of sight. When I saw who she was referring to, I stifled a gasp. It was the handsome Dr. Sparrow. *So he does live here.*

Two more fire trucks arrived on the scene, blue and red lights shining on our faces. Murmurs swept through the crowd. Slowly, those who were really pressed for sleep dragged themselves to the hospital to grab a bed in one of the call rooms. Gnawing on my lower lip, I felt anxiety race through me. I would never be able to rest well in a call room.

I checked the time on my cellphone. It was 10:36 p.m. I was thankful that Deb had handed me the gift of being off all the next day, which meant I could stand in front of the building a little while longer. Maybe we would hear something soon.

"I can't take this anymore," Sarah said. "I'm going to the hospital. By the way, the hot guy keeps staring at you. I would claim him before he's persuaded to divert his attention elsewhere."

My heart beat quickly as I watched her saunter off all cutesy-like. She was hoping her stroll would make Dr. Sparrow rip his gaze from me and paste it onto her.

I'd been avoiding looking at Sparrow, so I couldn't confirm whether he had succumbed to her powers of seduction.

Look and see, Pen, part of me kept saying.

Forget about him, my other side said.

Then an optimistic thought came to mind. If

Sparrow was tied up in a relationship with Sarah, then perhaps he would be a lot nicer to me. But picturing the two of them making out feverishly made my chest feel heavy.

"When are they going to come out?" a guy named Claude asked.

I hadn't noticed him standing beside me. I glanced at him then watched what he was observing. One by one, others peeled off from the crowd and headed toward the hospital.

"I guess I should go too." He turned to me. "Are you coming?"

I gazed down the street toward the hospital anxiously. The thought of sleeping in one of those hard beds in the call room made me feel nauseated. I could stay in a hotel. I had the money Aunt Christine sent me each month.

"Dr. Ross," someone with a mesmerizing voice said. I recognized the speaker right away. Not only that, but I could feel the excitement his nearness inspired within me.

Slowly, I looked up to see Dr. Sparrow, who was at least five to six inches taller than I was.

I swallowed nervously. "Yes, Doctor." Gosh, he was so gorgeous. I had to remind myself to blink or else he would think I was some sort of psycho.

Sparrow narrowed his eyes at Claude, who nervously shifted his weight from one foot to the other. Claude and I both got the message that Sparrow wanted to speak to me alone.

"Okay, well… I'm going," Claude said, walking away with his head hanging.

Then it was just the two of us standing so close that I could feel the heat emanating from him. The fact that he smelled so good made me further notice his black pants, which fit him nicely, and his soft cashmere cream V-neck sweater. I wondered if he was just returning home from a date. I also spotted certain onlookers pretending they weren't noticing us together. Sparrow was new meat, and that meant his mere presence teased everyone's curiosity. And I hated that my body betrayed me by reacting to his deliciousness. My vagina throbbed, and my nipples stiffened, reminding me how long it had been since I'd had sex, and not just sex but good sex.

"If you're looking for a place to land—"

I shook my head adamantly. "I'm just going to stay in a hotel."

"I know a place where you can stay for the night. It belongs to a friend of mine, and it has all the accoutrements of a five-star hotel and more." He raised his eyebrows when he said *more,* and I nearly choked. *No way, Pen. Stop being attracted to the man who's been more of a douchebag than a nice guy.*

"Everyone, listen up," Jamie, the leasing manager, said loudly enough to claim my attention.

I stopped staring at Sparrow and set my gaze on her.

"There was a fire in the basement. As a precaution, we're not letting anyone in until we know the building is safe and secure."

I rubbed my neck. *Am I flushed?*

"I heard people are heading to the hospital," she continued. "Thank you for that. We'll figure out ways to reimburse you for this night of not being able to live in your condos." She sounded so tired. "Oh, and make sure you log on to our Facebook page, where we'll be posting hourly updates, and I'll text all tenants when I get the all clear for your return."

"Jamie, come on. What about me? I don't work at the hospital," a guy named Pete groused.

"I can set you up in one of the call rooms," Sparrow said.

I did a double take, surprised he had the fortitude to be so charitable, or the pull.

Pete nodded as if he were an obedient robot.

"That'll be nice. I don't have the extra cash for a hotel."

"And anyone else who needs a bed tonight, let's go to the hospital, and I'll get you one," Sparrow, the man who'd only arrived days ago, said.

Chatter broke out in the group. I was still dead set on staying in a hotel room for the night or as long as needed. I could afford it. Then Sparrow took me by the hand, and I felt a business card in my palm.

"Go here," he whispered in my ear. "It's within walking distance. The doorman will be waiting for you."

I was still holding the card as I watched him lead the rest of the tenants down the street. He was like the Pied Piper. They were all so fixated on him that nobody noticed me remaining behind, confused about what to do next.

CHAPTER FIVE

PENINA ROSS

Sparrow's friend's place, which had all the accoutrements of a five-star hotel, was only six blocks away, standing where the financial and warehouse districts merged. The neighborhood was way more upscale than the one where I lived. I checked the address three times.

"Is this an apartment building?" I whispered.

It didn't look like one. One side of the ground floor was a bank. I hadn't reached the main entrance yet, but I was sure Sparrow had sent me to a place where it was too late to enter. I didn't know if it was my distrust of him or my instincts, but I wanted to turn back and just get a room at the W Hotel or something. However, I wasn't the type to give up without following all the way through. Plus,

Sparrow was an attending. If he asked why I hadn't stayed at his friend's place, I wanted to be able to say that I'd tried but wasn't able to gain access.

I made it to the front doors, and to my surprise, they did have a doorman, who was wearing a red suit with yellow tassels on his shoulders. He smiled when he saw me, as if he was indeed expecting me. Then he pulled the door open.

"You must be Dr. Ross," he said.

"I am," I said quietly.

He pointed toward the lavish lobby, which had black marble floors with gold swirls throughout the grain. The walls, the chandeliers, the French carved gold leaf mirrors, and furnishings were all finished with real twenty-four-carat gold.

"This way, ma'am."

As soon as I walked inside, he took fast steps to position himself ahead of me. I followed him past the ivory columns and white marble statues of Frenchmen from centuries past. But it was the ambiance that got to me. It felt as if I were walking across the bridge that led to heaven. The air was the perfect temperature, not too cool because of the warm night.

"This is your private elevator, Dr. Ross," the doorman said then asked me to press my finger on a touch pad and not remove it until the outside of the mechanism glowed green.

Even though I noted that he sounded as if he thought I would be back, I did as he asked. The doorman programmed a string of numbers and letters into a keypad, the outer ring of the touch pad beeped and turned green, then I removed my finger.

"You're all set, Dr. Ross."

My head felt woozy and my mouth, heavy. The environment was so comfortable that I wanted to fall asleep where I stood. I didn't have the energy to explain that I would only be spending one night in wherever I was going, so we said our final good nights.

The elevator smoothly climbed up the building. The numbers counted upward to the penthouse floor, and when the doors slid open, I was taken aback by the sheer scale and extravagance of the space.

I'D BEEN WALKING DOWN MARBLE-FLOORED HALLWAYS with high ceilings, passing signed contemporary art pieces that looked expensive. I peered into four enormous bedrooms, which contained large beds made-up with fluffy and luxurious bedding, sleek furniture, and floor-to-ceiling windows, which showcased killer views. Next, I peeped my head inside a grand salon that had a full bar with its own illustrious city views, a fully equipped home theater, a dining room with a huge table and leather chairs and a crystal chandelier above it. I made it to the kitchen, which nearly took my breath away. It had expensive appliances, tall white cabinets, two side-by-side subzero refrigerators and chef's ovens, warming drawers, a cappuccino station, a tall wine refrigerator a and a long marble island with a tall arrangement of fresh flowers on top. A card with my name on it stuck out. I pressed my hand over my mouth and gasped into my palm. After a moment of being immobilized, it was as if I'd been given a shot of adrenaline as I darted over to open the envelope. A handwritten note was inside, but it wasn't Sparrow's writing, because I had observed his handwriting earlier while reading his charts.

Thank you for saving a life. Please make yourself at home. In the main living room by the telephone, there is a menu for twenty-four-hour room service. Order whatever you like. Personal essentials are in each bathroom. However, if you find that something is missing, please call the concierge, and they will accommodate your requests. J. Sparrow.

I couldn't pick my jaw back up, at least not yet. What a surprising turn of events. But the jury was still out on whether he was a dick or not. People were complex. Every bad guy had a good side, and every good guy had a bad side. It was the percentages that determined their character. Something told me that in the upcoming days, I would get to learn all there was to know about Dr. Sparrow. Yet for the moment, I chose the bedroom with the white duvet on a king-size bed with a cherry wood frame. The room also had luxury carpeting, two cozy upholstered chairs in front of an electric fireplace, and a long dresser with a large mirror above it. The space felt inviting, as if it called my name, which was why as soon as I stripped out of the clothes I had put on in a rush, I climbed into the bed, curled up under those luxurious sheets, which felt like heaven against my skin, and went straight to sleep.

I GASPED AND SAT UPRIGHT, HAND AGAINST MY CHEST, catching my breath. I thought I'd heard something and felt a presence near. However, as I looked around the room, I had no doubt I was alone. I'd slept so hard that I had to take a moment to remember exactly where I was and how I'd gotten there.

"Sparrow," I whispered.

I had bitten the bad witch's poisoned apple, or in the case of Jake Sparrow, the wizard's apple. I wanted to crawl back under the comfortable linens and close my eyes, allowing the fuzziness to ease out of my head, but I was so eager to go on a deeper exploration of the penthouse that I pushed the covers off me and sat up on the side of the bed.

"Whoa, Nelly," I said and sat still until the wooziness went away.

When it was gone, I opened the curtains to let the afternoon light in. Wow, what a magnificent view of the city it was. I stood there for a while, watching traffic shoot down the street and the river flow in the distance.

Then my phone beeped, alerting me that a text message was waiting for me. I located my cellphone in the bottom of my purse. I had a text from Jamie, informing tenants that the fire had been started by an electrical issue, and because of that problem, we wouldn't be able to return for at least another twenty-four hours. She apologized for the delay but would make herself available to answer any questions.

I groaned as I rolled my eyes. Truth be told, I wasn't missing my place much after the night of sleep I'd had.

Then I saw a second text message from Dr. Sparrow. It wasn't shocking that he had my number. I was sure he'd found it on the list of neurosurgical residents.

Stay as long as necessary. J. Sparrow.

I wanted to respond with the first thing that came to mind, which was *You must have very rich friends.*

Then I had to stop and ponder. *Why the sarcasm, Pen? What do I actually want to voice to him? What is it about the whole ordeal that makes me so uncomfortable and grateful at the same time?* Then the answer came to me.

Are you the friend this swanky place belongs to? I typed.

My heart was beating fast as I stared at the send button. I had such a good thing going on there. Then I caught a glimpse of the time on the screen.

I inhaled sharply. It was 2:05 p.m. I had slept for over fifteen hours. *Holy shit.* I hadn't done that since before medical school. Suddenly, I felt so energized.

I could've skipped to the hospital and worked another full shift plus night call. Yet I didn't have to report to my shift until 5:45 a.m. the next day.

So I scratched my head, thinking. *Do I want my snarky question to offend Dr. Sparrow and make him ask me to leave?*

I took in a deep breath through my nostrils in an effort to control my impulses, and as I forced the air out, I tapped Send. Once my sassy question hit the airwaves, I hurried into the kitchen to scavenge up something to eat. As soon as I stepped into the spectacular space, I gasped while coming to an abrupt stop.

"No way," I whispered.

I so wish I hadn't sent that message.

Warm chafing dishes held a delectable continental breakfast of scrambled eggs, bacon, and blueberry crepes with a side of chilled cream. Another fresh bouquet of flowers was on the island. The previous night's bundle had been white roses, but the new ones were pink.

Then my phone dinged. *Shit. He replied.*

"Please don't make me leave," I repeated.

I pulled my shoulders back, ready to take the consequences of my actions like an adult.

. . .

The penthouse belongs to a friend. Enjoy yourself.
J Sparrow

All the tension in my body released as I sighed with relief. I could stay. I shook my hands thankfully above my head, eyes to the sky. *Yes, I can stay.*

CHAPTER SIX

JAKE SPARROW/ASHER CHRISTMAS

I focused on Si's hand. Around the hospital, everyone knew him as Simon Brown, chief of surgery. His fingers were pinched together, and he shook them as he said, "Are you out of your mind? Have you gone bonkers for shit?"

I settled deeper into the hard leather sofa, arm stretched across the top, legs spread wide, feet planted firmly on the ground, trying to convince him I wasn't sweating what he should've been concerned about. I had made a mistake by inviting Dr. Ross to the penthouse. The thought of her roaming the halls made me eager to get home for once. I wanted to see her—no, I needed to see her.

"It's already done, Si," I said. "Plus, I can handle her." I sounded overconfident, but I knew better than to interact with a woman like Penina Ross without having my guard up.

Dr. Ross was one of the most beautiful women I'd ever laid eyes on. Sensuality dripped from her pores. I wasn't that guy whose dick got tight every time he spied an exotic and natural seductress of her caliber, but her come-fuck-me quality was unmatched. I was shocked as hell to be that drawn to her when I first saw her walking toward me. Every woman I'd been in a relationship with came with a warning sign I'd seen at first sight. Crazy was in their eyes, proving they were indeed the windows to one's soul. Penina hadn't possessed the same quality, though. It was usually women like her I ran away from, fearing commitment and accountability. And before I'd seen her, I wasn't looking to get involved with another woman, not for a long time.

Si had suggested I take an apartment in her building to help blend in with the others.

"A single doctor, new in town, would live in the boarding hold, at least for a couple of weeks. We maintain a furnished, temporary apartment. Stay there. Show your face. Blend in," he had said.

I sniffed. "The boarding hold? That sounds like a fucking roach motel."

Si tossed me a key. "You're on the top floor. Give

it a look, then move your shit in there, and be happy, Ash. Oh, sorry, Jake."

I hadn't smoked in ten years, but the apartment, which wasn't that bad but not my style, was freshly painted, and whoever had done the work left a pack of cigarettes and a lighter on the counter. Living in a small place like that with not even my ex-girlfriend, who was more of a friend than a lover, to keep me company, made me want to have a smoke for old times' sake.

I bet Dr. Ross thinks I fucking smoke. I don't smoke.

"Did you just say you can handle her?" Si scoffed.

"I am handling her," I replied.

"Dr. Ross isn't a bimbo."

I sniffed bitterly. That was a fucking low blow, and we both knew it. Si was drawing a comparison between the sexy doctor and my ex, Gina Jones.

I shifted out of my relaxed posture to sit on the edge of the sofa. "Let's leave Gina out of this."

Si pounded the top of his desk. "No, Gina's not in this whole fucking scenario. It's my ass on the line here, Ash." Then he poked a finger in my direction. "Not yours. You're a fucking billionaire, Dr. Sparrow. But me?" He jabbed himself in the chest. "I get exposed for helping you change your identity, and I lose my fucking career. I worked hard for it—fucking hard for it."

Silence fell between us. He knew bringing up my money was a sore spot for me and why. The longer I'd gone without being a Christmas, the happier I'd been. The world knew what kind of depraved soul my father, Randolph Christmas, was. The man was dead, but his sins against the weak, vulnerable, and young lived on. No one had to say they suspected I could be like him. I looked into their eyes and saw that I was guilty by association. Sometimes, I could have sworn I saw the judgment in Si's eyes too. Maybe I was a coward, but I couldn't live with that, constantly knowing people were wondering how much like Randolph I was.

"Don't forget that I worked hard too. And I'm one of the best neurosurgeons in the world, and you know it," I said, wanting him to admit it.

His face tightened as he examined me. "I know it," he said finally.

I nodded sharply. "And Gina isn't a bimbo. She's a fucking survivor. And don't worry about Dr. Ross or your career. I'll take the hit before I let anything happen to you, and you know that too."

Simon clenched his lips as he shook his head

continuously. Fear was in his eyes, and I wished I could lend him some of my confidence.

Si and I had met at King's Crest Academy, a boarding school in Connecticut. Despite its name, the place wasn't built to be easy. Each day was supposed to feel as though we were being made to slog through shit—expensive, high-class shit. If I were more like my sister Bryn, I would've started brawls, landed myself in trouble, and embarrassed the family, and that would've made my father bring me home to be schooled. But living in the family mansion, a place I loathed, was different for a girl than for a boy, slightly more bearable. Our father behaved as if Bryn didn't exist. I, on the other hand, a boy, a son, was clay for him to mold into a weapon so that he could acquire more financial and political power. It was Bryn who had given me the most valuable advice I'd ever taken. It had gotten me through the four years at King's Crest and helped me become a person I wouldn't have been without it.

"Make friends with outsiders, not those fucking cunt boys whose parents are afraid of Randolph. You'll never be able to trust them. If they don't know anything about you, then you can feed Father the shit you want him to believe."

Simon Brown was a brilliant kid from England

who had been accepted on a scholarship. I later learned that he grew up as an orphan. Since he had no fucking parents, I thought that made him luckier than me. Before his arrival, I heard talk of boys wanting to crack the outsider's head open and serve his brains to the birds. Fuckers who were angry because they couldn't please their fathers liked to run in packs and push around the weak. The problem was that Si wasn't only a fighter, but he had more authentic confidence and smarts than every boy at the fucking school put together.

Our friendship began on the first day of school in biology class. The teacher told us to pick a partner for the semester. As I roamed the room, focused on the outsider, I could see my classmates eyeing me, hoping I would ask one of them to join me—too chickenshit to ask me themselves. I walked to the far corner of the room and stopped in front of Si's desk. The outsider sat with his back straight, chin high. It was as if he knew the second-smartest kid in the room would know to approach him. Truth be told, I didn't even know I was that clever at the time. It wasn't until we got busy, pushing each other to be our best, that I realized my IQ was above average.

"Want to be partners?" I had asked.

At first, Si tensed up, gripping the side of his desk. Then he sat up straight, composing himself.

"Don't bring down my grade," he said.

"I won't," I replied quickly.

He shrugged nonchalantly. "All right, then. I'll take you," he said in his bold English accent.

I sat beside him. For the first time ever, I didn't feel like a Christmas. I felt normal. I had two older brothers and two sisters, one whose existence I'd learned of six years ago. But Si was a friend who was more like the brother I would've chosen.

But there I was, locking eyes with my friend seventeen years later. He'd been keeping my secrets since our first year at the academy. He had none, while I had enough for the both of us.

"All right, then," he said, sounding much like he had when he let me be his lab partner. "Don't fuck this up, Ash."

Sighing, I stood. "I won't." I couldn't promise I wouldn't fuck up my world, but I could without a doubt make the promise to not blow up his.

Si nodded sharply, letting me know that he was solidly putting his trust in my hands.

I STILL HAD TWO MORE SURGERIES ON SCHEDULE FOR the day, a neuroendoscopy and a craniotomy, each to remove a tumor. As I walked down the hallway, head held high, I felt satisfied, knowing that I was a neurosurgeon and not a CEO. My father never would've let me be who I was. When I told him I planned to go to medical school, he shook his head adamantly and said, "I can't use a doctor. Maybe a chemist for our product development interests." Then he walked off.

But my father had a guy he thought he could control. I had the same guy, who operated in both our interests—Jasper, one of my older brothers, made sure I got what I wanted despite Randolph's demands. I graduated from the academy a year early thanks to keeping up with Si academically then went straight to university. As an undergrad, I double-majored in chemistry and biology. After I graduated, my father thought I was working as a manager in product development for United Alliance Laboratories Chemicals, one of Christmas Family Industries' conglomerates, but I was in medical school.

I was twenty-eight and nearing my fourth year as a neurosurgical resident at the University of California, San Francisco, when my father died on Christmas Eve. We were all in the mansion together, ready to play our roles for another bland holiday of parties, photo ops, and lies. Once he was dead and buried and unable to vex the world again, I decided to disappear.

Jake Sparrow was not a fake name, as far as I was concerned. Dr. Sparrow had done his fellowship in neurosurgical oncology plus advanced endoscopy and open-skull surgery in Australia. Si was the one who was able to get me into the program with my forged documents and no questions asked. As I said, Si had nothing to worry about. I wasn't going to get caught. I started inquiring about legally changing my name. The problem was that I couldn't do it without revealing my identity. The only person that could make sure I wouldn't have to do that was Jasper, and I wasn't ready to contact him yet.

Finally, the care station came into view. My team for my next surgery was gathered there. However, I couldn't take my eyes off one of them. *What the fuck is she doing here?*

I walked faster, and the first thing I said when I reached them all was "Dr. Ross? What are you doing here?"

"I… Um…" Her face was red, and I relaxed a bit. I didn't want her to think I was a prick.

"I asked if she could come in for this surgery. Dan had an emergency," Deb said as she walked past us.

Fucking Deb had a point to prove. She was going to keep throwing Dr. Ross on my service until she knew I wasn't being a dick to her resident.

The way Dr. Ross was looking at me, wide-eyed, with her succulent lips parted, had already made me fucking hard. *Fuck!*

"Dr. Sparrow, I promise. You want me on your team."

I stood speechless as my chest fluttered. My stunned gaze glossed over my team members as I wondered if any of them had a clue what was going on inside me. I couldn't be in the same OR with her, cutting on a patient. If Penina Ross was in the room, then she had all my attention. It was weak and unprofessional of me, but at least I was man enough to admit it to myself. One day, we could probably operate on a patient together, but that day wasn't then.

"Dr. Ross, follow me," I said curtly.

I took off without knowing if she was behind me. After I cleared the station and was heading down the sterile hallway, I could hear her footsteps. *I should fuck her now. I want to fuck her now.* I couldn't. But I had to make her understand. She needed to go back to the penthouse and relax.

"Dr. Sparrow, I wanted to thank you for your hospitality," she said. Her tone was unsure. "The flowers were gorgeous."

I didn't turn around. I couldn't speak. We walked across the ramp that led to the doctors' offices. I took my keys out of my pocket before I reached my door. My heart banged like a broken radiator.

I fumbled with the key until it sank in the keyhole. Her anxiety overtook me. I hadn't wanted to make her nervous, but I needed her to understand. I opened the door and waited for her to walk past me. When she did, my insides ignited.

Then I closed the door.

CHAPTER SEVEN

PENINA ROSS

I jumped when the door slammed. *What is up with this guy?* He'd shared his home with me, and I'd thought he would be nicer that day, more inviting, but he was the same dick I had faced from day one.

I folded my arms defiantly. "I'm sorry, Dr. Sparrow, but…"

"Be quiet," he whispered then turned away from me.

I closed my mouth immediately as I leaned back, shocked that he had said that. "I don't…"

"Quiet!" he roared, rubbing his temples.

I had to restrain the desire to say, "No, you be quiet." But I could see how vexed he was. Maybe for me it was a listening moment and not a fighting one.

So I pressed my arms tightly to my sides, opening myself up to hearing whatever made him not want to be in the same OR with me.

He finally looked at me again. Then he cleared his throat. "I'm attracted to you," he whispered.

My eyes grew wide, and I realized he was examining my reaction.

"I can't have you in the OR with me. Not yet. Go home. I'll talk to Deb."

I didn't think my voice box could work, but I said, "I can't go home, remember?"

"My place," he said in a rush. "Go to my place."

"I thought it belonged to a friend."

His jaw dropped. Then all of a sudden, I was in his arms, and our lips were pressed against each other's, our tongues swirling around each other, and holy shit, his cock was like a steel pipe against my belly.

The longer we kissed, the more my sex tingled and throbbed. I could've passed out from desire. Then he took me by the wrists and raised my arms above my head as his mouth abandoned mine. Dr. Sparrow's tongue and lips caressed my neck and earlobe as he rubbed his erection against my pussy, causing orgasmic sensations to spark beneath my mound.

I moaned and sighed, wanting so much more.

"Penina," he whispered, his warm breath filling my ear.

"Huh?" I sighed, dazed.

"Go the fuck back to the penthouse. Now." Then without warning, he moved away and darted out of his office and into the hallway nearly as fast as lightning.

I rubbed the side of my neck, where his lips and tongue had last kissed and tasted.

"My… did that just happen?" I asked breathlessly.

It had. It actually had.

It was not easy giving up my space in the OR. I was a surgeon and desperately wanted to see the great Dr. Sparrow in action and perhaps acquire a few new techniques.

Are we going to have sex any time soon?

I was lost in my own world as I shook my head, returning to the call room to sign out for the day. I remembered being in the office with Dr. Sparrow, making out with him, feeling his cock against me, wanting him so much that I could burst. *Am I in lust with the new attending?* Absolutely. But for me to love him, he would have to change and in a major way. He would have to be less moody and weird and more consistent. But still, it all seemed so surreal. I couldn't believe that of all people, it was I who had a physiological effect on the sexiest man in the world.

"What are you smiling about?"

I stopped simpering at the floor and looked up at Court, who was grinning while walking in my direction.

Wiping the smile right off my face, I nodded briskly as I passed her. I had forgotten how angry I was with her until then.

"Oh no, you're mad," she said.

I came to a halt then closed my eyes, composing myself. Her whiny and pleading tone, which was probably how kept women spoke to their sugar daddies, was annoying. Once the irritation she incited within dissolved, I folded my arms and walked over to stand beside her.

"Court, believe me, I want nothing to do with Rich. That's why I broke up with him," I said, keeping my voice contained.

Each passerby watched us inquisitively. By then, just about everyone knew Court was fucking my ex-boyfriend. Thank goodness I wasn't the type to get rattled by gossip. I'd grown up having to be emotionally stable or else perish. What others thought about me belonged to them and not to me.

"But you and I," I continued, "were supposed to be girlfriends. Put yourself in my shoes. It's hard to trust you anymore."

"Oh," she said, collapsing her shoulders as if she were the most innocent girl in the world. "I'm so sorry. I really am, Pen. We can't help who we fall in love with, right?"

I looked off to roll my eyes. She had said the same thing when she and Rich cornered me in Bellies the other day. Then I focused in on Dr. Sparrow speaking with Deb. The chief resident didn't look happy, but finally, she shook her head and shrugged.

Then my gaze connected with Deb's, and she waved me over.

"Listen, I have to see what Deb wants," I said, walking away from Court. "We can talk about it later." I shook my head. "Or maybe not. It is what it is."

"But are you still coming to the party? I hope so!" Court said.

Shit, I forgot about that. I was struggling to come up with an answer while walking backward. I saw

Court's eyes grow wide at the same time I slammed into something tall, strong, and hard.

"Oh," I said as large hands squeezed my waist. I recognized the scent of his breath next to my face.

"Sorry. Are you steady?" Sparrow asked. His cock of steel was against me.

I gulped nervously as I nodded. "Mm-hmm."

"Dr. Sparrow, you're coming, too, right?" Court asked, sounding more like a giddy Valley girl than usual.

He still had ahold of me. "Unless I'm called in. If not, I'll be there." His hands slid down my hips before releasing me. Our sweltering gazes were fixed on each other for a moment as he walked past me and continued up the hallway.

"I'll send you my address, or should I just write it down for you somewhere?" Court asked while keeping up with him as he walked.

Goodness, she was like an overexcited puppy and would undoubtedly trade Rich for Sparrow in a nanosecond.

When I reached Deb, she let me know that I was off for the rest of the day and thanked me for coming in.

"I just don't know about him. I don't think he

likes women. Whatever." She shook her head and walked away.

It was always hard keeping up with Deb. She was always skirting from here to there, putting out fires. I wasn't sure if she liked being chief resident, even though she was great at it.

I had it in my mind to tell her about the flowers he'd twice left me, but that would reveal that something intimate was going on between us. I couldn't even tell her about his cock. Each time I'd gotten close to it, it had been as hard as a rock, and that for sure was a telltale sign that he liked women, or at least his dick did.

CHAPTER EIGHT

PENINA ROSS

After leaving the hospital, and while walking to the penthouse, I received a text from Jamie, informing the third-floor tenants that we could come get some essentials if we needed them, but the building must be vacated by six p.m. Once again, she apologized for the inconvenience and asked any displaced tenants to let her know. So I stopped by my place to retrieve my laptop, two clean sets of clothes, six pairs of fresh panties, a few bras, my deodorant, and my special French lilac body cream, which I only used on those rare occasions when I pampered myself.

As soon as I stepped into the penthouse, all the tension drained from my body. The action was involuntary. Something in the air relaxed me.

I stripped out of my clothes and drew a warm bath in the large claw-foot tub, which was attached to the master bedroom suite, then slipped into the water. I had been on the verge of indulging in a bath earlier, before Deb called and asked if I could come in for one surgery. The difference between then and now was that I had a clearer understanding of how Dr. Sparrow felt about me. It was crazy and amazing how excited I'd gotten just by kissing him and having his hands all over me. I fanned my fingers across the side of my neck and let the tips slide down my skin. His lips and tongue had been there. His kissing and licking with the right amount of suction felt so erotic and delicious.

I slapped myself on the back of my hand, and beads of water dotted my face. "No, Pen."

Sparrow might want to fuck like rabbits, but he was an attending. I had gotten through almost seven years of residency without being the subject of a scandal. One month, one week, and three days, and I would be done. It was not the time to ruin my impeccable reputation.

AFTER BATHING, I DRIED MY SKIN THEN SAT ON A BATH

bench and massaged my French lilac lotion onto the parts of my body I could reach. I was luxuriating, sliding the cream up and down my legs, visualizing Sparrow's hands instead of mine.

Then I saw Sparrow moisturizing my thighs. I had packed condoms earlier, ten of them. I was thankful they were large enough to fit him. Holy hell, his bulge was huge. My vagina had cobwebs growing inside it. I hadn't had sex in a long time. I'd stopped banging Rich a day after he asked me if my pussy was itching, because his dick was. That was early last year. I had to remind him that I was the girl who always made him wear a condom.

"Your girlfriend, the one you're supposed to be loyal to, Rich," I yelled so loud, I felt like passing out.

He just showed me that stupid lost-puppy-dog look of his, the one he displayed when he was waiting for me to get over it and let the moment of contention pass so we could go back to business as usual. It always worked. I would shake my head and tell him I had to go to the hospital or something, telling myself that we were over. Then he would call me days later and relay a message from Caroline regarding the next family get-together or remind me that his sister, Blanche, was expecting us at her birthday party or something. He knew what his value to me was and used his family shamelessly to keep me. *And now Court gets Caroline, Ray, and Blanche as well as Rich's multitude of fun and interesting cousins, uncles, and aunts.*

I forced myself to stop missing Rich's family. The way I worked and my taste in untrustworthy men, made me fear that I would never have a family of my own. But I was too hungry to feel sorry for myself. I slipped into my oversized nightshirt then put on one of the many pairs of house slippers lined up under white robes hanging on a rack in the bathroom and sauntered into the living room.

I swiped the room service menu off the end table and plopped down on the comfy sectional sofa. "It was just..." I muttered to myself while looking off, focusing on nothing at all.

I never thought I'd be so interested in sex again after Rich. The cheating made me feel as if I wasn't sexy enough. Also, he had the worst roving eyes, which I always tried to ignore. Again, I had to shake memories of my complex relationship with my ex-boyfriend out of my head. *Why am I thinking about him anyway?*

"My intuition is warning me," I whispered.

There was something dubious about Sparrow. He had secrets—lots of them. Before we started making out, it seemed as if he'd confirmed that he owned the penthouse. I wasn't sure. I could hardly remember what we said to each other in those moments.

"No," I said, shaking my head vehemently. I would enjoy the day, but the next evening, when my shift ended, I would stay at a hotel if my apartment wasn't ready.

Feeling good about my decision, I picked up the phone and ordered a Cobb salad, a shrimp cocktail, and a bottle of sparkling water. While waiting, I checked my email. Usually on my days off, I would have a bunch of messages from other residents about patients. Since I hadn't had a handoff for two days, I only had about ten messages.

Suddenly, my Messenger started ringing, and when I saw who was calling me, I felt my face light up like the Milky Way.

"Zara?" I answered excitedly.

"Hey, Kit Kat," she said. "Sorry for leaving so abruptly. I needed to get the hell out of there."

I folded my legs and got a little more comfortable with my laptop. "Then you're not coming back?"

"Not to work. I have some loose ends to tie up in New Orleans, but then I'm moving."

My head jutted forward. "Moving?" I shook my

head continuously, hardly believing what I was hearing. "That's it? You're no longer a surgeon?"

She fell silent for a moment. "Well, no, Pen. It's not for me. I don't want to be stuck in a hospital for the rest of my life, and please don't say that things will change once we're attendings. I don't want to be an attending. I don't want to slice anyone's head open and dig out clots and cancer. I'm done. Got it, Pen? Done."

She was quite emotional by the end of her declaration. I couldn't say that I didn't know how she felt, because I did, only I saw things differently. Yes, I hated that I had to clear a blood clot or remove a tumor from someone's brain. I never took pleasure in having to do it, because I never forgot I was cutting on a sick person who never fathomed in a million years they'd be in that position. Empathy made me love what I did. Zara and I came from two different worlds. Her parents were traditional but rich. My mom had abandoned me emotionally even before Aunt Christine paid for me to go to boarding school at thirteen, and I'd never known my dad. I'd always felt Zara was way more entitled than I was and definitely spoiled. *Who drops out of residency less than two months before finishing?* Someone who didn't know what it meant not to have a solid cushion to fall back on, that was who.

"Okay," I said with a sigh. "Quitting is not the end of the world. It's the beginning of a new one, I guess."

"Yeah," she sang optimistically. "I knew you'd understand. You're the real deal, Pen. You're right where you're supposed to be. Now..." I heard her clap once. "The hot new doctor. Have you banged him yet?"

My gaze rolled around the large room with its heavy draperies and expensive furnishings. "What do you think?" I sounded pessimistic on purpose.

"My goodness, Pen, do you need a matchmaker? I can find you one."

"Ha," I scoffed. "Me? What about you? I haven't seen any studs coming in and out of your apartment either."

"That's because he lives in DC," she whispered.

"Why are you whispering?" I whispered.

"Because he's in the bathroom."

I momentarily froze. "You're not having an affair, are you?"

"Hell no. I'm a girl's girl. You know that."

I liked the firmness in her voice. I had known it. "Then why all the secrecy?"

"Because this is the first time we had sex. It was so… oh my God, Pen, I'm in love. He doesn't know it, but I'm in love."

"Well, Zara—"

"Got to go. See you one day soon."

"But I wanted—"

The call ended.

I thought she needed to hear that sex wasn't love, and that she should probably make sure her love wasn't born of oxytocin. Then I remembered that I might need to take my own advice at some point.

I yawned just as a buzz filled the air.

"Room service!" a woman's voice said, projecting through a speaker system.

I leapt to my feet and trotted over to answer the door. A pretty girl with long braids rolled in the food. When I told her I wanted to get my purse so that I could tip her, she raised a hand to stop me.

She remained smiling. "No tips from this room. It's all taken care of."

Then she wished me a good evening and walked out of the penthouse.

None of it would last. Good things never lasted. I would more than likely have sex with Dr. Hottie. We would fuck each other's brains out—that was for sure. Then we would talk and set the boundaries. He would have me out of his system, which meant we could perform surgeries together when the need arose. Perhaps we could be cordial with each other in social settings. We could definitely say good morning and good night. But we would never be able to be friends. He was too Jekyll and Hyde, good-cop-bad-cop, and angel-devil for that. Such a paradox, the man was.

I hummed as I took another bite of my salad. Each swallow made me increasingly tired. I wanted to stay up and wait for Dr. Hottie to come home, but earlier, I'd read the board and saw that he had four procedures scheduled. That meant he would be home late, and I didn't have the stamina to stay awake that long, especially after that bath.

Finally, I turned off my computer and carried it into the bedroom. First, I closed the curtains, then I set my computer on the dresser. I crawled into bed, yawned again, and not long after, fell asleep.

"Blue Butterfly" by Righteous Pearl blared through my phone. I sat up straight quickly, like a bolt of electricity had shot through me. After letting the song play while I scrubbed my face with my hands, I turned it off.

"My goodness," I muttered.

No daylight shone through the cracks in the curtains, and my bedroom door was closed. I hadn't done that. *Did Sparrow return home at some point during the night without waking me up?*

I flung my legs over the side of the bed and let my feet drop to the floor. The fuzziness cleared out of my head a bit more, and I forced myself to stand. That was one comfortable bed, and I was sure I had slept in it for the last time. My body yearned for its comfort, and because of it, it was taking me longer than usual to get into the mindset of going to work.

Is he here?

A surge of energy made me hop to my feet. Then I walked through the condo, poking my head in and out of rooms, seeing no sign of Sparrow. However, in the kitchen, another continental breakfast was set up, and that time, one long-stemmed red rose in a shimmering crystal vase sat next to the fruit platter.

CHAPTER NINE

PENINA ROSS

I stared at the rose with my mouth twisted thoughtfully before plucking it out of the vase. Something felt odd about the bouquets of flowers and the more intimate red rose. If Sparrow wanted to fuck, he didn't have to go through the hassle of such an elaborate seduction. *Has he looked in the mirror lately?* All he had to do was buy me a drink, sparkling water, of course, and bourbon wings then kiss my neck like he did the other day. There was something about a man who would do so much to land a girl in bed. I suspected he was a chaser. That meant that once I was caught, he would be done with me. I had to remember that as well as consider that he was an attending.

I had no time to give it more thought. I rushed

back to the bedroom, stuffed the rose into my bag, planning to confront him with it, then got dressed. After my shift ended, I planned to return to Dr. Sparrow's penthouse—I knew for certain that it belonged to him—and collect my things. Then that would be it. No more kissing, dry humping, or neck nibbling.

My heart fluttered, and my pussy wept as I thought about his lips on my skin.

"No, Pen," I whispered, darting out of the bedroom. "It's only physical." I had to put an end to whatever we were doing before we got too emotionally involved with each other. I ran the risk of falling hard and fast for Dr. Sparrow. Something about him felt familiar.

My first stop was back in the kitchen, where I wrapped a warm croissant filled with blueberry sauce and cream cheese in a napkin. I also took some sliced oranges and grapefruit. A silver urn was beside to-go cups, and I filled one of the cups with coffee, added cream, and rushed to the private elevator. On the way down, I reminded myself once again to say no to any sexual contact with the sexy doctor, even if my body said yes.

I FELT A SENSE OF RELIEF. SPARROW WAS IN SURGERY, so I didn't have to see him for a while. That rose was burning a hole in my bag, though, and we had to talk about it. At least I had more time to form my words.

My morning routine hadn't changed. I signed in then finished drinking my coffee, which was very good, and read prep notes and patient records from the previous night's handoffs along with new cases. Angela and Jude wanted to know for certain if Zara had quit. Even though I knew the answer, I wasn't one to impart information someone had shared with me without their permission. Then the conversation quickly turned to Sparrow.

"He's so damn good-looking," Angela whispered, trying not to be heard by anyone not involved in our conversation.

"I heard the guy was gay," Jude said. "So don't get your hopes up."

My brow furrowed as I looked up from the computer screen at him. "Who told you that?"

"It's well-known." Jude dropped off his stool. "The guy's gay, so don't embarrass yourselves by coming on to him."

I could tell Jude wanted me to let his claim about Sparrow stand, but no way was I going to do that. I spun my chair around to watch him dig through his locker. "I hadn't heard that. So who told you?"

He smirked. "Why? Are you planning on joining the soup line of starving alley cats?"

"Ouch," I said, shrugging a shoulder. "Saint Jude sounds jealous."

"Ha," he said, not looking away from his locker. "Whatever. All of you girls are going crazy over a guy."

I grinned slyly. "Oh, so you *are* jealous?"

He slammed his locker shut. "Jealous? What do I have to be jealous about?"

Jude used being a doctor as sexual capital. He often left with a new woman after his shift. On many occasions, a girl who appeared to be in her early twenties ate lunch in the cafeteria with him. He kept a steady trail of females, each hoping he would choose them to be the surgeon's wife.

Zara used to swear Jude was a virgin. I never asked her to prove it because I didn't care. He wasn't my type. He was too overworked—he wore too much hair gel and too much cologne, he plucked his eyebrows, and I could have sworn he wore eyeliner. But the worst part about him was that he avoided the OR as much as possible.

"Do you really want us to answer that question?"

Angela asked, laughing as she finished tying the shoes she wore for the second half of her shift. She said changing shoes kept her feet healthy.

"Dr. Ross, somebody wants to see you," someone called.

We whipped our heads toward the guy standing in the doorway. I tried to place his face, but I'd never seen him before.

I pressed my hand on my chest. "Me?"

"Are you Dr. Penina Ross?"

"Yeah," I said.

"Then yeah. You."

I sat up straight, knowing whoever was looking for me could've been anybody, but I hoped it wasn't Dr. Sparrow—or maybe I hoped it was.

THE GUY WAS A FIRST-YEAR SURGICAL RESIDENT AND said his name was Oscar. Someone in the ortho program greeted him, and I thought perhaps I'd been assigned to one of their patients who needed a neuro consult. I believed that even more when I walked over the bridge that led to the attendings' offices.

I knocked on the office door of Dr. Rocco Best, who was an ortho attending.

"Come in," he called, his voice muffled by the door.

I cautiously opened the door and stepped into his office. My eyes grew wide. Instead of the doctor, my ex was sitting on the small sofa.

"Rich?" I asked, making sure my eyes weren't deceiving me.

Simpering, he stood slowly, rubbing his palms on his jeans. "Hey, Pen."

"Is everything okay?" After all, he was a quarterback and once had taken such a big hit that the pain in his knee was over a seven for an entire month.

"I just wanted to see you," he said.

I shook my head rapidly. "Why?"

He took a deep breath. "I miss you."

I leaned away from him, frowning. "Miss me how?" He was with Court, and six days ago, they'd stood side by side in a strong show of new-couple bliss.

"When I saw you at Bellies, I just… I miss you."

I closed my eyes and sighed. My ex, the consummate cheater, wanted me to be the woman he cheated on his current girlfriend with. When I opened my eyes again, I was sure he felt the fire of my anger burning him alive.

"Why don't you just stay single, Rich? That way

you can fuck whoever you want without screwing with a poor girl's heart."

He jerked his head back. "*Your* heart? You broke *my* heart."

I was even more confused. I hadn't said *my* heart. "No, my heart is fine. I'm over you."

"Well, I'm not over you."

Shit, he's approaching.

"You're so fucking sexy, Pen. I miss your lips and your body," he said.

I took steps backward, pinning my backside to the door. He narrowly missed taking me in his arms. I shot both hands in front of me, signaling for him to come no closer.

"Rich. Stop."

"I loved you. You were never around, never fucking available. And you're the one that stopped having sex with me."

My mouth fell open. There was no way I was going to let Rich put the blame of our deficient sexual relationship on me. "That's because your dick was itching, and I wasn't the cause of it."

"What was I supposed to do?" he asked as if he hadn't heard me. "I had needs. I'd rather have met them with you, though."

A cynical laugh escaped me. "Are you kidding me?"

"That mole on your waist." He sipped air sharply between his teeth. "Shit. I want to kiss it."

My neck jutted forward. My being trapped in a doctor's office with him felt so wrong, but I knew Rich well enough to know he wouldn't cross the line with me, so I wasn't in danger.

I clapped loudly to wake him out of his lustful haze. He was staring at my body as if he could see through my scrubs.

"Rich! Wake up!"

He blinked hard, and his gaze landed on my face.

"We broke up. We're over. You cheated on me. And yes, I wasn't there for you. We don't work. But I'm sure there are enough sexy groupies in the world ready to fuck you and even some with a mole on their waist."

It happened so fast. I was in his embrace, being carried across the floor, then my back hit the sofa. Rich's tongue invaded my mouth when my jaw dropped in surprise. His dick grinded against the hood of my pussy, and his hand pushed its way toward my clit.

"Just one more time, baby," he whispered against my mouth. "Please."

My right knee was free, and if I angled it to the left, my kneecap could've collided with his hard dick, but instead, I turned my face away from his. "Rich? Are you forcing yourself on me?" I made sure my tone was calm but firm.

He stopped trying to kiss me and leaned his head back. "What?"

"I'm under you, and I never gave you permission to bring me here," I said, keeping a pragmatic tone. That was the best way to help him reason himself out of a heightened state of desire.

"Shit." He scrambled off of me. "No, I wasn't forcing myself on you. No."

I rose to my feet quickly, moved to the door, and opened it. "Goodbye, Rich." I hurried into the solace of the hallway.

"Pen?" he called after me.

I stopped in my tracks but not in response to Rich. My eyes met Dr. Sparrow's curious gaze.

Then Rich stepped out of the office behind me. Sparrow looked at him then downward, checking out Rich's boner. I was not going to show the sexy doctor how mortified I was that he had seen us that way. I pulled my shoulders back, ready to walk right past him. However, Sparrow turned away from me first as he put his key in the lock and disappeared into his office.

"Who's that?" Rich asked.

He was right behind me, careful to not touch me. Anyone could see him out in the hallway. The hospital had eyeballs everywhere, which was why he'd had some guy who was not in my ward come collect me and bring me to him.

"As I said, goodbye, Rich."

I clutched my stomach and got the hell away from the scene as fast as I could. Why do I feel so nauseated? It was as if I had lost Dr. Sparrow, even though I was resigned to putting distance between us. But I didn't know if that was what I wanted. I didn't know anything anymore.

CHAPTER TEN

PENINA ROSS

My shift ended. I hadn't run into Dr. Sparrow since our encounter in the hall of offices, and I was sort of disappointed about that. I wanted to know how he would've treated me after that, and I definitely wanted to explain exactly what he'd seen. I did not have sex with Rich, which should've been evident by Rich's boner. If I had banged him, he wouldn't have had a hard-on. Surely Dr. Sparrow would know that. After all, he was a doctor.

The apartment building wouldn't be ready until the next morning at nine a.m. Hospital personnel that lived in the building were staying in pretty nice call rooms on the west wing of the facility. Apparently, no one had known the space even existed. My fellow tenants prattled on about how nice the call rooms were. I asked Kevin, who lived in our building with his wife, Lulu, who was a nurse, if there was a bed available for me. He said space was tight, but if I showed up, somebody would find one for me.

That was the sort of person Kevin was. He went above and beyond to make the impossible happen. I thanked him and settled on staying at the W Hotel since that would be no hassle at all. Plus, paying homage to Dr. Sparrow's luxury penthouse, I wanted the high-class suite and first-class room service.

So once again, as I walked to Sparrow's place, I passed on my regular order of bourbon wings at Bellies. Robert, the doorman, let me in. We fell into a short conversation about my being a neurosurgeon.

"I still can't believe it. You're too fine to be so smart." He giggled at his own sense of humor. "You're supposed to be kept by one of these high-rolling motherfuckers living here."

I tossed my head back and laughed, knowing he truly believed in the logic of what he said. But I couldn't be offended by his remark. A doctor should know that it took all kinds to make the world go around. Finally, I told him goodbye and rode the elevator up to the penthouse.

I forgot to ask him if Dr. Sparrow was home, and

I even forgot to check the board to see if Sparrow was in surgery. Although I didn't want to run into him, I also did. He needed an explanation about what he'd seen between Rich and me before I packed my things and vacated. If he was attending Court's party the next week, then he would know that Rich was her boyfriend. I didn't want him to think I was the sort of woman who fucked around with men who made commitments to other women—even if the man didn't practice upholding his side of the bargain.

Once again, I appreciated how smoothly the elevator doors opened. Everything about the penthouse felt sleek.

My phone beeped twice as I walked to the guestroom, and I sighed exasperatedly as I tossed my bag onto the bed. I searched through all the junk inside until I found my cellphone. The first message was from Jamie, stating that the fire inspector had found that the electrical wiring of the building made it unsafe. All tenants would be reimbursed the previous month's rent in order to find lodging for the next seven to fourteen days while the building was being rewired. The only thing that kept me from groaning with disappointment was the second message I received. It was from Dr. Sparrow, and it simply read *Stay. J. Sparrow.*

I sighed, scratching my head, then tiredly fell on top of the bed and tried to figure out what I really wanted to do. I could say, "Thanks for the hospitality, Dr. Sparrow, but no, thanks."

Flipping onto my back, I narrowed my eyes at my phone. I had several things to ask him, like whether he was staying at the penthouse or I was the only resident there. I also wanted to just say what he'd seen earlier wasn't what it looked like. But maybe he had no suspicion about what had gone on between Rich and me at all. As far as he was concerned, Rich was a patient, and I had just ended a consultation. Dr. Sparrow had nothing to be skeptical about unless I tickled his curiosity.

Thanks, Dr. Sparrow. I'll stay, I typed and hit Send.

He immediately responded with a thumbs-up emoji and told me to order whatever I wanted for dinner.

You're not joining me? I replied before I realized what that question must look like to Dr. Sparrow. It almost sounded as if we were in a relationship. But he was just an accommodating attending, rewarding me for saving one of his patients' lives.

I sat up, believing that he was going to ignore my last question, but my phone dinged.

I have surgeries.

I decided to leave it at that, but then I changed my mind.

Need help? I added a smiley face for good measure.

No.

I felt gratified by his quick response. Rich had rarely replied to me with such swiftness. He liked to make everyone who needed something from him wait. I always believed it had something to do with him being a professional athlete. When people were willing to kiss his ass just to be near him, he derived a sense of satisfaction by making them anticipate his reply, even his girlfriend.

Deciding to think of my ex no more, I forced myself to stand then went into the living room to order a shrimp po' boy salad and hot mint tea with lemon. Room service informed me that they would be up in eight minutes with my order.

"That's fast," I said.

"You have express service, ma'am," the woman said.

After she said that, I was done vacillating about

whether to enjoy the gift of the luxury accommodations. I would remain in the penthouse until he asked me to leave.

I nearly skipped to strip out of my clothes and put on the fluffy white robe and slippers, then I sauntered back into the living room. As I gaped at the view of the buildings sprawled across the city below, which was kissed by the Mississippi River, I suddenly realized it was the first time I'd ever witnessed such a sight from a place I was living in. A neurosurgeon could make a lot of money to one day afford a place like that, but I'd never pictured myself being one of those people. I wasn't in it for the money.

The doorbell rang, and I quickly went over to answer it. It was room service, and she once again reminded me that I didn't have to tip.

I sat at the table and ate as much of the salad as I could before my eyelids became too heavy for me to stay awake. It was time to wrap myself in the most comfortable bed linens that had ever touched my body. So I rolled the silver food cart out into the hallway, hopped into the shower attached to my guest room, and once I towel-dried my skin, crawled into bed and went straight to sleep.

I was awakened by "Double Dare" by Jan Wilder. It was the song my alarm played the mornings of my on-call days.

Goodness, I was counting the days to the end of my residency. I didn't know what it felt like to have a vacation, but I planned to take one in August. I hadn't decided where to yet, but I suspected it would be somewhere tropical and exotic. I moaned as I dragged myself out of bed. At least I'd slept comfortably again.

After getting dressed, I found the standard continental breakfast in the kitchen but no flower. I'd forgotten all about the red rose I stuffed in my bag. It had gotten lost with all the other shit I hauled on a daily basis. I couldn't help but feel that Sparrow was sending me a message and had indeed thought something sexual had occurred between Rich and me the day before.

I wasn't late so I ate one of the blueberry-glazed-and-sweet-cream-cheese-filled croissants, some apple slices, and some bacon. Next, I put coffee in a to-go cup and added cream. Then I got in the elevator and headed down.

As I walked the path I usually took to the hospital, passing Bernard's Bakery, I ran into Eloise, who was on the sidewalk, setting up a sign promoting their summer buns, which were melt-in-the-mouth flaky pastries filled with cinnamon-encrusted pecans, warm caramel, and a butter-rum ganache. Each bun was over eight hundred calories, which was why I never ate more than one a month.

"Penina, is that you?" she asked, spotting me before I said something first.

I waved. "Morning, Eloise. It's me."

We hugged.

After we released each other, Eloise put her hands on her hips. "Where's Zara?"

I turned down the corners of my mouth. "She's not with me this morning."

"Is she okay?"

"As far as I know." My tone rang optimistically.

The nosey baker smiled, and I knew she was pressing me for the same information my colleagues at the hospital wanted to know.

"Well, you know that missing Christmas brother?" she asked as I checked my watch. If I stayed a full minute, I would be late.

"Huh?" I asked, distracted.

"One of my customers said they spotted him around here."

I wanted to get my feet moving as fast as possible. "Spotted who?" I asked, feeling my frown tug at my temples.

She flapped her hand, waving me away. "Go, sweetheart. You hospital people are always in a rush."

That was exactly what I did, practically running the rest of the way to the hospital.

My day began as it usually had. I logged in to the EMR system and did handovers, then I started rounds, then Deb sent me to float in emergency, where I ended up performing an aneurysm clipping that took four hours and a craniotomy to drain a hematoma. Next, I repaired a ruptured blood vessel, which took three hours. I was going on eight hours with only a turkey-and-cheese sandwich that I scarfed down between procedures along with two juice boxes. I hadn't seen Dr. Sparrow all day, either, and was sort of relieved about it.

I sat out on the patio of the fourth-floor terrace

with Angela. We both needed fresh air, food, and a moment to talk about anything but work. She had just told me about her call with Zara.

Angela checked over her shoulder to make sure no one was listening then leaned toward me. "I think she's getting married," she whispered.

My jaw dropped so fast and low that it could've hit the floor. "You think?"

She shrugged indifferently. "She sort of alluded to it."

I scooted to the edge of my seat. "What does alluding to getting married sound like?"

Angela threw her hands up in surrender. "I don't know, but don't bust my balls, okay?"

I sat back and relaxed as much as I could. "I'm not busting your balls. I just know Zara's not the marrying type."

She checked over both shoulders. "I never thought she was the type to quit the program when she only had one month to finish."

I raised a finger. "One month, one week, and one day, actually."

Angela had been frowning at something behind me, so I turned to look. When I saw, I quickly faced forward.

"Why is Dr. Sparrow always staring at you that way?" Angela asked.

He was with a man and a woman. I presumed one or both were related to a patient of his. We often brought consults or family members on the terrace to deliver updates or treatment plans since the seating, the sun, and the view of the water made it such a pleasant place to be. My head felt floaty, as I couldn't stop thinking about how he hadn't looked away even when our gazes met.

I shrugged indifferently. "He doesn't like me so…"

She tilted her head. "Do you really think that?"

"He doesn't want me in on any of his teams, and he has the most severe cases, which means I could learn a lot from him." I didn't feel a need to mention that I knew why he felt so uncomfortable in the OR with me.

Angela rolled her eyes. "You don't need to be on his team, Pen. You're a fucking awesome surgeon. Fuck him. Even though he's amazing, you could still probably teach him a thing or two."

I snorted a chuckle.

Then she abruptly scooted to the edge of her seat. "He's still staring at you. Tell me the truth. Have the two of you screwed?"

"No," I said emphatically. *Not yet at least.*

She kept watching him with her hand hiding her mouth. "He doesn't even know he's doing it."

I patted the table. "Well, you're staring at him, too, so eyes on me."

"You don't care," she said as the corners of her mouth lifted in a tiny smile.

"I don't care about what?"

Her eyes narrowed to slits as she studied me. *Holy shit, Angela is figuring it all out.* Regardless, I wasn't going to tell her that he'd taken me to his office, and we'd kissed like two sex-starved individuals. And I sure as hell wasn't going to tell her that he had been putting me up in a luxury penthouse in the business district.

"He's coming," she said and nailed her back against her chair.

Of course, she didn't do as I said and continued gazing at him.

My heart ran a hundred-meter dash when he appeared at the edge of our table. Then we both watched him inquisitively.

"Good afternoon, Dr. Baker," he said to her and waited for her response.

She gulped. "Good afternoon."

Then he looked at me, and butterflies fluttered in my stomach. “Dr. Ross, good afternoon.”

I nodded. *Shit, say something.* I cleared my throat. “Dr. Sparrow.”

“I heard about your two surgeries from the ER. Good work.”

“Thank you.” My voice was too high-pitched for my liking.

Without another word, he walked away, and we couldn’t take our eyes off him until he was out of sight.

Angela sank deeper into her seat, releasing all the tension from her body. “Where the hell did he come from? It’s like he’s not even human.”

I grunted cynically, thinking about some of our run-ins. “Oh, he’s human.” I shot to my feet and gathered the plastic from the sandwich I’d devoured along with an empty bag of chips because I had rounds to make. “I have to go.”

She stood too. “So do I.”

And that was the last time we spoke for the day.

THE ER WAS BUSIER THAN USUAL THAT NIGHT, AND before my shift ended, I had three more emergency surgeries. On my way out, both Deb and Chief Brown mentioned that they wanted to talk to me about a fellowship. Chief even walked me to the exit, pitching all the benefits of taking up my fellowship at Unity Memorial instead of Boston. I wanted to ask him if he was giving me the full-court press because he'd heard from Boston. *Have they accepted my application?* But I didn't ask. I still didn't want to know.

Before walking to the penthouse, I stopped by my place and checked my mail. It had the test results from a DNA test I had taken back in March or April. I had forgotten all about it. I had taken the test because I was hoping to find connections to relatives on my father's side of my family. And maybe I would score the gold medal and find out who my sperm donor was. I felt more nervous about seeing those results than learning whether I would be moving to Boston at the end of my residency or not.

My fingers were crossed that Sparrow would be inside when I entered the penthouse, but he wasn't. I even searched each room to confirm his absence. I was too tired after that long, arduous shift to eat right away, so I stripped off my clothes and went straight to bed.

I WOKE UP AROUND MIDNIGHT TO PEE. MY STOMACH growled, so I dragged my tired body into the kitchen. A single white rose wrapped in gold leafy paper and a note card were on the island. I immediately hurried over to read the card.

This was missed with your breakfast.

J. Sparrow

I FELT MY ENTIRE FACE COLLAPSE INTO A FROWN. That was just super weird. The only time he'd spoken to me was on the fourth-floor terrace. We shouldn't let others know we were flirting with each other, falling into some sort of hot and heavy relationship, but he could've at least sought me out other than just running into me on the patio to say hello, good morning, or good night.

I smelled the rose then found a tall glass, filled it with water, and placed the beautiful flower in the liquid. Then I ordered room service before going back to bed.

My next two shifts were again action-packed. I saw Dr. Sparrow three times in one day and six in the next. On each occasion, he pretended as if I didn't exist. And I hadn't ended up on his service yet. However, each morning, there were roses with my breakfast. The guy was the master of mixed messages.

It was day four of living in the penthouse after getting the message that my apartment wouldn't be inhabitable for seven to fourteen days. All had gone just as it had on the previous day, only at the end of my shift, on my way to the care station, I ran into someone else I wanted to avoid in the hallway.

Court slapped both hands on her cheeks. "Oh my God, there you are," she said, rolling the *R* sound on her tongue like a Valley girl. "I've haven't seen you in, like, forever."

I forced a smile. "Actually, I saw you earlier this week." I didn't want to talk to her since I was ready to finish handoffs then go to Sparrow's penthouse, order food, and go directly to bed.

"Listen," she said, taking me by the arm in a friendly way. "Rich and I were talking, and I thought Greg Carrol should be your date for the party. What do you think?"

I was already out of work mode, reserving what

was left of my brain power for handoffs. So I was barely able to process what she had said. "Who?" I asked.

"Greg Carrol? Tight end. Hot guy. He saw you before, and he's into you."

I glared at her. "No." Although I sounded tired, there should've been no doubt I meant what I said.

"Hello, Court," Dr. Sparrow said from behind us.

The sound of his voice made me jump before I turned to face him.

"Hi, Dr. Sparrow. I was just talking to Dr. Ross. I think she should go on a date with a hot football player. Don't you?"

I wanted to faint or, even better, be transported out of the moment.

"Only Dr. Ross can answer that question," he said and winked at me. "Good night, ladies." Then he continued up the hallway.

Court and I watched him go.

"That man, that man. My God, he's so hot. So hot." She rubbed the back of her neck as if Dr. Sparrow had just made her feverish. "Anyway, where was I? Right. Greg Carrol."

I ripped my gaze off Dr. Sparrow and snapped a hand in front of my face to stop her. "I said no."

"Come on," she pleaded, back to her charming little Valley girl act.

I had no time for it. "No more fucking athletes," I said and continued my journey to the care station.

I thought I would find Dr. Sparrow there, charting or following up on a patient, but I didn't.

I searched the area a few times, taking my time finishing up, wondering where he was.

CHAPTER ELEVEN

PENINA ROSS

As soon as I stepped out of the elevator and into the penthouse, the smell of delicious food flowed up my nostrils. It was definitely seafood—lobster or scallops. Music played softly as well, a light jazzy instrumental.

"Dr. Ross, is that you?" Sparrow called from the kitchen.

My eyes expanded like balloons. He was there.

"Shit," I cursed under my breath then cleared my throat. "Yeah." There was no nervousness in my voice, even though the feeling consumed me.

"I'm in the kitchen. Come join me."

My heart fluttered. I quickly looked down at my crotch. *Pussy, no.* She had jumped, getting excited about him being so near.

I could feel him waiting for me as I walked down the hallway and into the living room, which had a view of the kitchen. He was standing at the oven with a drying towel draped across his shoulder. When I got close enough, he turned, and immediately, his pale-blue eyes roamed over me.

He leaned on the large marble-top island. "Are you ready to eat something?"

I jerked my head back. "Did you cook?"

He smirked. "Yes. I cooked." He sounded and looked proud of himself.

He cooks too.

"But you left the hospital not too long ago."

"What was your answer?"

I frowned. "Answer about what?"

"Are you going to be Greg Carrol's date?"

Rolling my eyes, I said, "Absolutely not."

He smirked as if he was satisfied by my reaction.

Finally, I realized we were staring at each other. I had to blink to be released from the power of his captive gaze.

"Did you make scallops?" I asked without taking one step toward him.

"Yes, pan-seared and zucchini pesto pasta." He pointed his head in the direction of the bedroom I'd been sleeping in. "Go, put your things down, then come back and join me at the table."

"We're going to eat dinner together?" I knew I looked as nervous as I sounded.

"That's the plan."

His smirk was so enticing. It made it difficult to remember why I was so upset with him. "But you never talk to me at work."

"But you know why that is."

My brow furrowed. "No, I don't."

He snatched the towel off his shoulder then tossed it on the marble. I stiffened as he moved toward me until our faces were close.

"Must I remind you why I can't engage with you at the hospital—right here, right now?"

My head spun like a top. I thought I said, "Okay," before getting the hell away from him, actually running like a frightened cat to the bedroom.

My heart was speeding as though Mario Andretti was driving it. I could still picture the way he looked at me. *What is happening to me? I'm attracted to him, like really attracted to him. And what are we doing together?* That night had to be the night we defined our relationship or lack thereof. We also had to resolve the sexual tension between us. At some point during the evening, we had to fuck. It didn't have to take long. He would stick it in, we would bang, then that would be that. He would be done with me, and I would be done with him. *Done.*

"After dinner, sex," I whispered then yawned. One more night, and the next day, after my shift, I would make a reservation at the hotel—maybe.

Dr. Sparrow plated dinner beautifully on white porcelain dinnerware, he'd filled a gold basket with various types of dinner rolls, and a gold dish of sliced butter sat next to it.

I tilted my head and gave him a suspicious look. "Did you really make this?" I could hardly believe it.

He gave a short nod. "I did. I wouldn't lie about making dinner."

"Well, you've already lied about owning this place," I said, and I immediately wanted to take back those words. I was tired and uninhibited.

"Let's sit," he said, obviously choosing to ignore my accusation.

Sparrow walked to one side of the table, where a plate was set. He had on a white V-neck T-shirt and loose cotton lounge pants. His magnificent cock, visible through the material, pistoled down his leg. It was hard and not being carefully constrained by his underwear. He looked down at where I was staring. I quickly zipped my eyes back to his face.

He shrugged. "I already told you. It's the effect you have on me. It'll pass. Sit."

He still held my chair out for me. I didn't want to get too close to his wiener. I was creaming in my panties. *Say it, Pen.* I wanted to tell him that we should go to the bedroom and get it over with already, but instead, I walked over to sit in the chair.

When we were close, we locked eyes. I saw the question in his. He wanted to do something to me—touch me, kiss me, *something*. But instead, I sat, and he helped me scoot my seat closer to the table. I couldn't look away from him as he took the seat across from me.

We kept staring at each other, neither of us picking up forks to dig in.

"It smells good," I said.

"Thank you," he said breathlessly. "Who was he?"

I frowned, confused, ready to sleep, dig in to that amazing-looking food Sparrow had made, and fuck. "Who are you referring to?" I stifled a yawn.

"The guy you came out of the office with."

"Oh, him." I thumbed over my shoulder because it was the only gesture I could come up with at the moment. "That was… um…" I didn't know what to say.

His frown turned severe. "Did you fuck him?"

"No," I said, shaking my head adamantly. "He's my ex-boyfriend, and now he's with Court. You know Court, who we just ran into again in the hallway."

"She's with your ex?" he asked as if it were the most disgusting thing he'd ever heard.

I tried not to smile, even though I was happy he was on my side. "Yeah," I said with a sigh.

His glare picked me apart. "And you're not happy about it?"

I shrugged. "He's a serial cheater." I saw no need to tell him that Rich had been trying to fuck me seconds before he saw us.

"He wants you still," Sparrow said.

Finally, I picked up my fork and spiraled zucchini pasta around the tines. "But I don't want him."

He nodded forcefully. "Good."

Don't look at him. Don't look. Pen, don't look.

I put the forkful of pasta into my mouth, and the flavors of fresh basil, garlic, pine nuts, and parmesan ignited my taste buds.

"Mmm," I said, eyes closed as I chewed.

When I opened my eyes, he was watching me as if he was conflicted about something.

"What?" I asked.

He coughed to clear his throat and readjusted in his seat. "Tell me, why did you choose to become a neurosurgeon?" He sounded so formal. It was clear we were on a date without him officially asking me out on one.

"Because it's the top of the food chain and I had to prove I'm worth a damn," I replied. Jeez, I sounded bitter. As soon as those words left my mouth, I pressed my lips together. I'd never revealed that to anyone. It wasn't the whole truth, of course. It was just the answer that came out of me because of exhaustion.

I cut a plump scallop in half with my fork and shoved the delicate and sweet meat into my mouth. As I chewed, I wondered why he was looking at me with such a severe frown.

"You're worth a damn," he finally replied.

"How do you know? You barely know me." *Shit... again, wrong thing to say, Pen.*

He smirked sort of naughtily. *Whoa, my panties are melting some more.*

"I asked around. Deb says you're her best resident. She's anxious about you finishing the program.

She's used to counting on you," he said.

I was watching him with that faraway look in my eyes. I was choked up. I hadn't known Deb felt that way about me.

"Then you saved Trey Sharp's life. He's been asking about you." He cracked a smirk. "His friends want your number."

I chortled. "I'll take a date." I'd said that because I wanted to see his reaction.

"You're on a date," he said.

We grinned at each other. My head felt floaty and my heart, light. *Say something.*

I ripped my gaze from his face and put it on one of the perfectly browned scallops. "What about you? Why did you become a neurosurgeon?"

"Same," he said.

I looked at him again. "Same?"

"Same as you. I wanted to prove I was worth a damn."

"To whom?" It was probably a question he should've asked me, but I'd thought of it first.

"Myself," he said. "What about you?"

Why am I smiling? "To my mom, who is MIA, and to a father I never knew." *Shit. Why so fatalistic, Pen. Stop!* I took a drink of the glass of bubbly mineral water next to my plate. "Sparkling water," I said with surprise.

"Room service informed me that's what you like to drink," he said.

I snorted cynically. "So what is this?" I turned my head slightly. "Like a chase?"

"A chase?" he asked. I suspected he was feigning ignorance.

"You know, you're the guy who likes the chase, the catch and release." I could already feel the dread of him releasing me after fucking me, because I was certain I was going to let him fuck me.

"I'm not a chaser, Penina," he said.

I wanted to fan myself, but I couldn't show him how flustered I was by the way he said my name. I had always hated the sound of my full name but not anymore. He had just made it sound as sexy as hell.

"You're not a chaser?" My high-pitched tone had gotten away from me—to bring it back, I took another drink of water.

"I'm not. I like you."

"What do you like about me?" I asked, not believing him at all.

"You're classy. You have a natural elegance. You're smart. Kind. My patients rave about you."

"They do?" I asked quietly.

He cracked a smile. "You like rounds."

"I do." I could hardly believe he'd noticed.

"You're sexy. Very sexy."

I was having a hard time breathing evenly as we stared at each other with fire and desire.

Then he shifted abruptly in his seat. "Penina..." he said as if he'd realized he pronounced it too gracefully earlier and wanted to take it back. "That's an odd name. Do you know how you got it?"

I sniffed bitterly. "Yeah, that's what you call the glob in your belly you never wanted or liked from the get-go."

His sexy smile transformed into something more sympathetic. "I'm sorry to hear that..."

When he trailed off, I could tell he wanted to call me Penina again but thought better of it.

I raised a hand. "It's okay. Really. I'm being overly fatalistic this evening, which isn't my style unless I'm past the point of exhaustion."

Dr. Sparrow smiled. "I don't like my name either."

I jerked my head back. "Jake Sparrow? That's the name of a leading man in a hospital soap opera." I hoped my smile showed him that I was being witty, but he looked off as if he was in misery. "Or not."

Suddenly, he put his smile back on. "So, Penina, how do you like your dinner?"

I was thankful that he'd changed the subject. "It's delicious. You're a good cook."

He scratched his forehead nervously. "Thanks, but it wasn't difficult."

I narrowed my eyes thoughtfully. "But aren't you exhausted? You're at the hospital and in surgery more than any attending I've ever known."

Again, that look of despair returned to his face. I suspected he was thinking about something, and whatever it was hadn't come from a happy place.

"Sleeping's difficult for me, Penina," he said in a strained voice.

"Oh." My body went rigid, and even though I wanted to eat another scallop, I felt immobilized by his admission. Not only that, but the way he'd said my name still made my heart flutter. I could hear him call me by the name I used to hate until he spoke it for the rest of my life.

"I want to make love to you," he said finally.

I blinked, surprised. Then I looked down at my plate, constraining a smile. "You waste no time getting to the point, do you?"

"You can say no," he said.

I didn't look up because the level of my desire

wouldn't let me. If I saw his face, I would toss my plate across the table, rip my clothes off, and laid my naked body before him, presenting myself as the night's dessert.

"Yes," I said as I lifted my face. "Yes." I needed to repeat it just in case he had any doubts how much I meant it.

CHAPTER TWELVE

PENINA ROSS

Our gazes stayed stuck on each other. He rose. I dropped my fork and stood too. We kept staring at each other as we moved along the table. It was as if my feet were on autopilot and I was having an out-of-body experience.

Then we were face-to-face. So much yearning raced through me that I didn't know what to do next. Dr. Sparrow wrapped me in an embrace, and I freely let my body melt against his. His lips brushed sensually against mine as our tongues softly stroked each other. The more we kissed, the more our breathing grew faster and more audible.

My body felt light as air. Total satiety was carrying me off to another dimension. Then

Sparrow inhaled sharply against my mouth as he gripped my hips and yanked me against his firm cock. My lips still pressed against his, I gasped.

We stared into each other's eyes long and hard. I knew he was thinking what I was thinking. There was no turning back. What I had desired for days was soon to come. A lengthy and intense seduction had made the moment happen.

My breaths were heavy, causing my breasts to rise and fall against his solid chest.

His long fingers stroked the side of my face as he whispered, "You're so beautiful."

I sighed, feeling my breath warm my lips, and whispered, "Thank you."

So quickly, our mouths collided, and our tongues sank deeper into the flaming desire of each other's mouths. We kept kissing as he lifted me off the floor and carried me. Through my daze, I could perceive my surroundings changing from the dimly lit hallway to a dusky bedroom. It wasn't the one I'd been sleeping in, though. It was the largest room in the penthouse—the one in which I'd been looking for signs that Dr. Sparrow had occupied it while I was sleeping.

Dr. Sparrow guided me down onto the bed, spread my legs, and positioned himself on top of me.

His rock-hard cock slid up my slit, applying pressure on the most sensitive spots of my pussy. A sigh arose from the depths of my throat and slid softly past my lips. He groped my breasts through my blouse then reached his hand down my pants, fingers under the crotch of my panties.

I shivered involuntarily as his fingers glided in and out of me. "Feels…"

"I'm too…" he whispered, then tongued me deeply.

After Dr. Sparrow came up for air, he pulled my T-shirt over my head. As I tasted his delicious tongue, he feverishly unhooked my bra, freeing my tits.

"Damn it," he said, looking at my breasts as if he was overwhelmed by the sight of them. "You don't know how long I've wanted to…" His hot, wet mouth came down over the tip of one. He sucked and nibbled until his tongue gently laved my nipple.

Suddenly, he stopped and crawled off of me. "I'll get condoms. Finish getting undressed."

He took off toward the bathroom, and I quickly shed my clothes. Once I was completely naked, I kicked the duvet down to the foot of the bed. The heavy bedding was getting in the way of our sexual movement.

Dr. Sparrow came back wearing only briefs. My eyes widened at the sight of his chest. The sexy doctor was muscular without being overworked. He wasn't hairy either. Rich was like the abominable snowman. I hadn't realized how much I liked a guy who wasn't so furry until then. *And his bulge...* Shit, he must've had a horse dick tucked into his underwear. My pussy wept as I thought of his cock skimming my long-neglected walls.

He barely took his hooded gaze off of me as he sat the box of condoms on the nightstand. My mouth was caught open, and my body was left in suspense.

No more conversations needed to be had, and no foreplay was necessary. What was happening between us was pure sexual engagement.

My breaths hitched as he took off his underwear, freeing the thickest cock I'd ever seen. He'd already put a condom on it.

"You're large," I said.

Dr. Sparrow was too caught up in his lust to comment on what I had said. He got on the bed and positioned himself between my legs. Curling his arms around my thighs, he clamped them into place and slid his soft, warm, wet tongue over my clit.

"Oh," I cried and clawed at the tight sheets.

He instantaneously made sensations blossom like wildflowers through my pussy. He moaned as he licked. Right away, I knew he wasn't an amateur. Rich had a lot of sex with lots of women, but he wasn't as competent at rousing pleasure as the sexy new attending.

I made all kinds of noises, ones I'd never made before. The orgasmic sensations felt so velvety, so silky, and so intense. I ran my fingers through his hair and begged him not to stop then to please stop but also keep going. And he held me so firmly that I couldn't get away from his mouth.

"Oh!" I clenched my back teeth and swallowed.

I raised my head to try to focus on what he was doing, but I couldn't concentrate.

"Jake..." I whispered. *Shit, I called him Jake.* But I couldn't help myself. However, I wouldn't make that mistake again.

The sensations turned more intense, swirling through my pussy like a tornado. Then the orgasm bloomed. I cried out as my legs jerked. I wanted to call his name and refer to him as Jake again, but that would've meant we would be crossing the one line that meant we had decided to throw professionalism completely out the window.

"Ah!" I cried out again as it so quickly happened a second time. *What the hell.*

I was still shocked by the back-to-back orgasms as Sparrow eased over me. The way he proceeded was almost ceremonious as he separated my thighs, held his cock, and guided it toward my globe. My pussy quickened, surrendering to his will, as we kept our lustful gazes on each other. Then the point of no return arrived, and his shaft plunged into my depths.

I could feel every ounce of his magnificent girth, and I tossed my head back and croaked, "Oh."

More noises ensued out of me. I closed my eyes, allowing my nerves to feel him. In and out, he shifted, stretching my tight pussy to kingdom come.

I folded my arms around his neck and placed the side of my face against his. He thrusted. His sweet musk helped drive me to my peak.

"Oh my God," I cried unrestrainedly.

Because I was feeling it—really feeling it. It wasn't a neurological-brain-stimulation orgasm that occurred from all the emotions that were tethered to the act of having sex—being desired, feeling close to someone I was attracted to, and the exercise itself. No, it was a real physiological orgasm caused by the thrusting, his low moans, his hard body on top of me, and his fingers digging into the linens on each side of my head.

Harder, faster, rhythmically, he thrusted.

Holy shit. I had no idea a dick could make a vagina feel that way. My nerve endings tingled each time his cock brushed them.

I tilted my hips toward his movement. My body tensed as his mouth clamped down over mine and we kissed greedily.

"Oh my," I whimpered, wanting to call him by his first name, as a real intravaginal, penile-aroused orgasm threatened to surge through my pussy for the first time in my life.

Then he nailed me deep with his manhood and held himself very still.

"What?" I breathed heavily, still chasing his dick with my hips. I had awakened out of my stupor, disappointed that he'd stopped, and the climactic sensation disappeared.

"Wait," he whispered, fastening my hips to the bed. "I don't want to come yet. You're so fucking sexy. You're making me come faster than usual."

"I never thought I would come at all, not intravaginally, at least," I said breathlessly.

Suddenly his interest quickened. "What do you mean?"

He stared at me with a curious frown. Surely he knew what I was alluding to, but maybe not. I was starting to realize that Dr. Sparrow was one of those on-the-nose people who rarely let themselves read between the lines to find the true meaning of what was being spoken.

"I was about to have an orgasm before you stopped, and no guy I've ever been with could do what you just did. Even when you went down on me." That was a mouthful for such a moment, but I wanted him to understand me completely.

"Can we do this again and often?" he asked.

I tried not to chuckle. "Are you always this exact?"

"Yes," he said and began indulgently pumping his cock in and out of my pussy.

I closed my eyes and sucked air. "Fuck."

His mouth moved over mine, and we tongued deeply.

In, out, in, out, he moved. Orgasmic sensations returned just as fast as they'd gone away, and I directed the sensitive area of my pussy toward the action.

We kissed and groaned, and I felt unable to merge close enough with him.

"Oh shit!" he roared. His body tensed against me.

"I'm going to come," I announced.

He relaxed a bit, and I could tell he was trying to hold on for me. I wanted to climax intravaginally and prove that Sparrow was indeed a sex god.

Then it caught and spread through me like wildfire. My eyes expanded. I felt choked but still cried out to the Almighty as my pussy and thighs quivered.

When my body went still, Sparrow slid out of me, guided me onto my stomach, raised me by the hips, and set me on my knees.

"I'm going to fuck you like I did in my fantasy," he announced as he slammed his dick into my pussy.

I cried out as his tip hit my cervix. It ached so fucking good as he kept doing it repeatedly. He grabbed my hair and sucked hard on my neck, fucking me like a horny animal. I went happily along for the ride. He deserved to fuck me hard. He had made me come thrice in one session. I never came once with Rich, and only by accident with a few guys before him.

Then Dr. Sparrow wrapped me up tightly, and we collapsed onto the bed as he groaned and croaked in my ear, coming hard.

"Sorry to fuck you that way," he breathed. "I couldn't help myself."

I clenched my pussy around his dick. Even though it was spent, I could still feel it. Not only that, but I sucked air, able to squeeze my fourth orgasm out of it.

RICH WOULD HAVE BEEN DONE HAVING SEX FOR THE night after getting off, but Jake Sparrow wasn't. He repeatedly ate my pussy, making me climax in all sorts of exotic ways and many times back-to-back. He ran his hands all over my body, telling me how soft my skin was, making me shudder.

"You have all the right curves, baby."

That made me chuckle. No guy had ever told me that before. When Dr. Sparrow turned hard again, he slammed his cock into me again, which culminated with me coming intravaginally again.

CHAPTER THIRTEEN

PENINA ROSS

My alarm clock played the same song it had the other day, indicating that it was not an on-call day. As I blinked, waking up, I recalled a few details. First, I was naked. Second, I still felt moist between my legs. Thirdly, I was alone in bed. And finally, merely hours ago, I had experienced the most highly enjoyable sex of my life with Dr. Jake Sparrow.

I stretched my arm out and felt all the mattress beside me, making sure it was truly empty. It was. He was gone.

"Really?" I groused as I turned on the bedside lamp. He could've at least said goodbye.

Then a dreadful thought occurred. Maybe he'd lied to me. He had indeed fucked me and was done with me. I kicked myself for believing him. I knew better. On top of that, I had no time to cry or pout about it. My shift started in less than half an hour, which meant my alarm had been sounding off for thirty minutes before I heard it. That also meant that Dr. Sparrow had left the bed before four thirty. I trusted that he would've awakened me if he had heard the alarm.

I took a shower in his bathroom, which had the biggest shower I'd ever seen. No way would I go to work smelling like sex with an attending. Angela had a gift for not only smelling sex on someone but also identifying whom that person had fucked. She was right at least nine times out of ten.

Unfortunately, I had to make my shower short, knowing I would never have a chance to indulge in its opulence again. After drying off, I searched the floor beside the bed for the clothes I'd taken off before we made love. I didn't see them until I looked on the mustard-colored leather chair in front of the curtains. My jeans, T-shirt, bra, and socks were neatly folded on top.

I took a moment to stare at my garments. He had taken time and paid attention to make them neat for me. Perhaps he wasn't going to discard me like last night's fuck. I envisioned myself crossing my fingers and hoping not as I hurried over and swept them off the chaise.

Once I was back in the room where I put my things, I put on a fresh pair of panties. Then I stood up straight as I remembered that my panties from the previous night were still somewhere in Dr. Sparrow's room. But I had no precious minutes to spare to go look for them. I put on my shoes and grabbed the bag I usually took to work, which had days-old snacks in it. I didn't even have time to drop into the kitchen and see if a continental breakfast and another flower were waiting for me. Or perhaps I was too chickenshit to do it. As I stepped into the elevator, I knew what I felt deep inside. I couldn't help it. I believed Sparrow had gotten what he wanted, and charming me with beautiful flowers and five-star breakfast spreads was officially over.

The first thing Deb said to me was that I was late. I apologized profusely and reminded her that I was hardly ever tardy.

"You're right," she said as she walked off. "All's forgiven."

Then I groaned and slapped my forehead when I

saw my schedule. I was on call. *Fuck, my phone played the wrong song.*

On the walk over, I had decided to go through with moving into a hotel room. But I would have to wait until the next morning to get my things from Sparrow's penthouse. I hadn't seen him as I signed in, but I never saw him that early in the morning. Usually, he was either in surgery or prepping for it. I was happy to prolong our first post-sex meeting. I still wondered how he would respond to me. But I didn't ponder long. Handoffs had officially begun, and instead of Dr. Sparrow, I filled my mind with the patients who needed me.

"You had sex last night," Angela said, sitting at the station next to mine.

Fuck. "What?" I asked, sounding as if she were crazy for suggesting it.

"You had sex," she restated strongly.

"Who had sex?" Kevin asked.

"Nobody had sex," I said.

Then *he* walked into the care station. My eyes casually flicked away from Dr. Sparrow, who hadn't looked at me once.

"Dr. Baker, you're scrubbing in on an awake craniotomy," Sparrow said to Angela.

She jerked her head back. "With you?"

Her caramel skin was blushing. Sparrow threw his hands up as if to say, *Who the hell else?*

She patted me on the shoulder. "Maybe Dr. Ross. She's—"

"No. You," he said sharply.

When he turned his back on us and walked off, he still hadn't looked at me yet.

"Shit," she muttered under her breath.

I stopped staring at the space he left behind like a hurt child. If Angela wasn't so trapped in her own distress, she would've noticed my despair.

Clearing my throat, I pulled myself together. "Hey, why were you trying to pass off the surgery to me anyway?"

She twisted her mouth thoughtfully. "He's starting to make me nervous."

My chest felt tight. "Has he made a pass at you?" I was hoping he wasn't a serial cheater. Dr. Lumpkin in cardiology was one of those guys who'd gone through as many nurses and residents as he could when he first arrived at the hospital. I attracted those kinds of guys like shit did flies.

"No," she said, shaking her head. "There's something else. He has secrets." She gestured as though she were parodying an explosion. "Very big ones." Then she sighed as she closed out her computer.

"Anyway, I gotta go scrub in. At least he usually smells good." She winked.

I snorted. She didn't know how on the money she was.

At that point, since we'd fucked and he was acting weird again, I figured I was obligated to find out as much about him as I could. The fact that Nurse Krislyn Hardy was on my service felt like a blessing in disguise. Kris was a chatterbox who couldn't stop talking for more than two seconds whenever we weren't with a patient or in surgery. She knew everything and just about everyone in the hospital and probably New Orleans too.

We had just finished a consult and were walking to the coffee shop in the lobby for a twenty-minute break before seeing our next patient. I started by asking her how long she had known about Court and Rich. My goal was to get her started on the easier topics of gossip before easing her into the more restrictive ones.

She gave me a light stroke on the forearm. "Oh, Pen, I'm sorry you had to hear about them that way."

I felt my eyes grow wide as I finished paying for both our lattes—the drinks were on me. *What does she know about the way I heard it?*

"What are you talking about?" I asked.

We sat at a small round table. "Court let everyone know that you were hurt by the news, but despite it, you took it rather well. Personally, I never thought you gave a damn about the guy. He used to bring you all of those gifts, and you would just turn your nose up to them. That's why Court figured you didn't deserve him. But everyone knows he'd rather be with you. Even she does. That's why she's trying to hook you up with Leaky Penis, Greg Carrol. I mean, the guy takes antibiotics like they're breath mints."

I frowned. "How could you know that? He's a professional athlete. Don't they have team doctors to slip them anti-dick-itch-and-drip drugs?"

Kris searched the room, checking over both shoulders. Then she leaned toward me and whispered, "Dr. Best is their candy man."

I was learning more about the salacious shit that went on around the hospital than I wanted to know. I had to find a way to stop her from regurgitating more mindless gossip and get to the mindful stuff.

I leaned back in my seat to put distance between us. "To each their own, I guess. And as far as Rich is concerned, I've had several conversations with Court about how untrustworthy he is." I would never tell her how he'd tried to fuck me the other day. "She's made her bed. Now she has to lie in it."

"Yeah," Kris said with a sigh. "I agree."

Linda, the barista, called my name, and I got up to get our drinks. When I sat back down, Kris complained about how watery her latte was and went back up to the counter and made Linda make her a new one. I thought mine tasted fine. It wasn't sweet. I didn't like sweet coffee.

When she settled in her chair again, we only had seven minutes to talk about who I really wanted to discuss. So I went right to it.

"Dr. Sparrow. What's the story on him?"

Her eyes instantly grew wide. "Oh. Him." She grunted. "He's the one who opened up the west wing and got all of those beds for everyone. You know how much money this hospital doesn't have. We have a nurse shortage and not enough residents. Anyway…" She rolled her eyes as she shook her head. "I found out that someone bought the hospital, and now there's all this money. Then he shows up. And he's, like… spending it."

One reason Kris was so good at gossip was that she knew how to piece together the details. "How is he spending the money?" I asked, practically on the edge of my seat.

She shrugged indifferently. "He's paid a lot. And yesterday, I heard him tell Chief Brown to get him three more residents and a fellow. I mean, who the fuck is he?"

That was a good question. Unfortunately, the alarm on my phone blared, letting me know that I had five more minutes to make it to our patient's room and begin our pre-surgery consult.

"I'll tell you more later," she said as we both shot to our feet.

I didn't want to wait for later. "There's more?"

"Yes."

We walked down the hallway on our way to the care station to meet up with the rest of the team for our next consult.

"Just tell me a little now," I said.

"He made a—" She tensed up. "Speak of the devil," she mumbled.

I followed her line of sight. Dr. Sparrow was approaching us and beaming at me.

"Good afternoon, Dr. Sparrow," Kris said.

"Afternoon," he muttered without taking his eyes off me.

I was not convinced that he didn't know he was staring.

Kris chuckled after we passed him. "He's always staring at you," she whispered. "Everybody knows it. That's another thing. Deb reported it to the chief because she thought it was affecting his interaction with you, and she said the chief just blew her off. It's like he has so much power, but he's only an attending."

"But I heard his reputation precedes him," I snuck in.

We were almost at the care station, and Dr. Flanigan, the primary surgeon, was about to lead the team up to the patient's room.

"His reputation? No one knows his reputation," she said.

I chewed on her final words through our consult then the prep for surgery and even during the procedure. I wondered if Kris or anyone else knew that Sparrow was loaded or had rich friends in high places. I was determined that the next time he and I were alone, I would get some answers.

NIGHT CALL WAS HOT. WE WERE FEELING THE PINCH of the resident and nurse shortage, but another guy fell off his motorcycle, and I had to clip a brain bleed, irrigate, and remove the skull to relieve the swelling all in one surgery. Then, an hour before my shift was to end, another guy had a motorcycle accident and needed the same procedure. By the time I made it to the condo, I could barely keep my eyes open. I didn't even look for Sparrow. Instead, I dragged my tired, aching, and hungry body to the bedroom, fell facedown on top of the bed, and was asleep shortly thereafter.

CHAPTER FOURTEEN

PENINA ROSS

I woke up to something firm against my back, and something even stiffer was pinned against my ass. Then I felt his warmth and the electricity that raced through me whenever I was that close to Dr. Jake Sparrow.

"You're awake," he whispered, rubbing then planting a gentle kiss on my shoulder.

I only faintly remembered how I'd gone straight to sleep as soon as my body hit the mattress.

Then he nibbled my neck and cupped my tits as he continued rubbing his stiff erection against the crease of my ass.

"I need you, Penina," he soughed.

The taste of my tongue made me put a hand over my mouth. "I want you, too, but I could use a serious teeth brushing and a hot shower." The stress sweat from back-to-back highly challenging surgeries had made my armpits rank.

Dr. Sparrow steered me onto my back and peeled my hand from my mouth. I felt horrified as I watched his lips move toward mine and make contact. Our kissing was slow and erotic as his teeth dragged across my lower lip. Before we delved too deep in the act, he took his shirt off, and so did I. Then we removed our remaining garments so fast that we flopped back down on the bed to catch our breaths while staring into each other's eyes. My heart played like a fiddle.

"Why don't you speak to me at work?" I asked.

He opened his mouth then closed it.

"Are you ashamed of me?" I asked.

"You know the answer to that, Penina," he said finally.

"To what? Why you don't talk to me or if you're ashamed of me?"

"Both," he said as he reached over to retrieve a condom from the nightstand. I liked that he'd entered the guestroom prepared.

"If I knew the answer, I wouldn't be asking."

He glanced back at me as he rolled the condom

over his huge dick. "I'm your attending, and I'll never be ashamed of you."

The corners of my mouth drew up in a satisfied smile, but I wasn't done questioning him. "Do you own this penthouse?"

He positioned himself on top of me. Then he used his knee to part my thighs, and without pause, his erection surged through my pussy.

We kept our hooded gazes pasted on each other as he slid in and out of me, our bodies shifting forward and back with each thrust. Not until sparks of orgasm started to flicker down there did I close my eyes and suck air sharply into my throat.

Then his mouth melted with mine, and we kissed as our sexes continued to collide.

THE ROOM SMELLED LIKE AN AMBROSIA OF OUR SWEAT and breath. The atmosphere was unlit, yet our eyes had already adjusted to the darkness. Each one of Sparrow's strokes had felt so damn good up until the moment of his release. Fucking him was different from doing it with any man I'd ever been with. I couldn't even say we had fucked. The intense feelings that had been stirred inside me were like nothing I'd ever felt. It was as if with each crashing of our hips, we were in search of something bigger than ourselves. Without a doubt, all variations of our sexual exercise were the two of us making love.

I lay in his arms, fighting the urge to drift off. He stayed silent behind me. From his quiet and even breaths and the rigidity in his body, I was sure he wasn't struggling to stay awake.

"Thank you," he said and kissed the back of my shoulder then drew me closer against him.

"No, thank you," I said.

His hand slid up and down the curve of my hip. His touch held a yearning, and it made me want to fulfill his every desire to have me.

"Are you fighting sleep?" he asked.

I raised my eyebrows, shocked he had noticed. The thing was that I didn't want to lose consciousness. I wanted to be with him. Whenever I woke up, he was always gone.

"Why aren't you sleeping?" I asked.

"Haven't I told you that I don't sleep?" he asked.

I pursed my lips as I pondered his question. I faintly recalled him mentioning it, but I'd thought he was being ironic.

"You really don't sleep?" I asked then yawned.

"Rarely," he said.

"Are you a vampire? Because that would explain your unusually good looks."

He chuckled, something I'd never seen him do before, or at least not very much.

"No, but thank you, I think."

I chortled. "You're welcome. Then are you haunted by something?"

Silence lingered between us.

"We're all haunted by one thing or another," he said.

Dr. Sparrow was a master at evading a direct question. I was developing feelings for the guy and was standing on a very important threshold when it came to choosing to fall into a new relationship with a very secretive man or get away from him as fast as I could. So far, I was leaning toward taking a chance on him. But I needed him to start telling me the truth and fast.

"But what are *you* haunted by?"

Again, silence hung in the air until he said, "A lot."

"Could you be more specific?"

His hand slid from my thigh and into my pussy, and I seized his wrist.

"No," I said breathlessly. "I want you to pleasure me but not at the expense of you being completely honest with me."

He withdrew his hand and flipped onto his back. I turned to face him.

Dr. Sparrow stared at the ceiling for a long while. I had been trained to listen, so I knew to give him space to tell all he could.

"I like you, Penina. I don't want you to stop seeing me."

I snorted softly as I jerked my head. "Are we seeing each other?"

"You're here, aren't you?"

"Yes, but I don't even know what this is between us. And you still haven't answered my question. Why can't you sleep? What's haunting you?"

Again, silence.

"As I said, a lot," he finally replied.

I took a moment to consider his answer and compare it to the strained look on his face. His eyebrows were furrowed, and the skin between his eyes was puckered. Whatever he was remembering was causing him distress.

Gliding my hand across his strong chest, I said, "I have a lot going on in my past too."

He turned to watch me curiously, and I took his expression as an invitation to continue sharing.

"I always feel I need to prove I'm worth more

than the life my mother dragged me through. That feeling never goes away. All I can do is bury it, but it's still there. We neurosurgeons are at the top of the food chain." I cracked a tiny smile. "I mean, unless you're asking a cardiothoracic surgeon." I raised a finger pointedly. "Orthos and plastics have egos the size of Jupiter too."

His gentle smile matched mine.

"I can't tell you my past, Penina."

"Then you're hiding from it?"

He went silent again, and I closed my eyes and shook my head. He'd put me in an awful position.

"I don't think I want to be involved with a man who has secrets." I sounded unsure about my claim, but I kept my eyes shut, not wanting to be swayed by his convincing baby blues.

"I don't want you to be involved with any man. I want you to be involved with me." His finger slid gently down the side of my face, and I couldn't stop myself from looking at him. "I can promise you that whatever I'm keeping to myself can't and won't hurt you."

At least I knew that the instincts of Angela, Kris, and probably everyone at the hospital were on the money about him. He had just admitted that he had secrets.

"I didn't expect to meet you, Penina," he added.

I shook my head emphatically. "What does that mean? People are curious creatures. You do know that, right?"

"Yes."

"And just about everyone at the hospital is suspicious of you. Did you know that too?"

"Yes, but I do my job expertly. My patients don't ask where I'm from. They just want me to save their lives or improve the quality of their lives."

I studied the contours of his beautiful face as he gazed into my eyes. *How could a man who looks like that trust that he could drop off the face of the earth in peace?*

"Listen," I said with a sigh. "I'm not one of those women who has to shove you into a box where their hero is spotless and unhuman in order to feel safe. I grew up in chaos. Chaos is where I thrive. But it's tiring. I just want to know how it feels to be in a blissful relationship for once."

"So do I," he said. "Let's try it together."

My grimace made my forehead ache. *Did he hear a thing I said?* "I would think trying it together would begin with you telling me the truth, the whole truth, and nothing but the truth."

"I agree," he said, sounding diplomatic about it.

I narrowed my eyes shrewdly. "Then answer this... do you own this penthouse?"

"I bought it, but it doesn't belong to me."

The fact that he'd purchased it didn't surprise me. But I'd been correct about him—he was Mr. Moneybags.

"Then who does it belong to?" I asked.

He groaned as he gripped his skull and massaged his scalp. After a moment, he examined me. I guessed he was looking for trust in my eyes. I didn't have to make my expression trustworthy. If anyone could keep a secret, I could. Though I would've liked to have known why I was keeping the secret.

"I bought this place for a friend who's like family," he blurted then deepened his frown. "We grew up together."

"But this place is not cheap," I said.

He nodded, agreeing with me. "Right, but that's relative. New Orleans isn't Manhattan."

I smirked, thinking about how he always had an answer. I wasn't going to ask him how much it cost, because that would've been a classless thing to do. But I put it all together. Dr. Sparrow was rich, but he was a successful and single neurosurgeon. That meant he didn't have much to spend his cash on. As I recalled, he definitely had a place at the boarding hold, which wasn't the name of the building, but it was what everyone called it. It was the place we lived until we finished our residency or fellowship. Attendings usually moved in until they were fully settled at the hospital then abandoned the boarding hold when they found a more permanent residence.

Also, I'd shared about my family, and he hadn't done the same. I suspected his secret had to do with them, and I could understand not being ready to divulge all the shitty family secrets. So I decided to give him a grace period, though I didn't know when the time would end.

"Okay, well, thanks for answering as much as you could. Now, I think I should take a shower while I can still stand."

He reached over to run his finger around my areola. "Call in for tomorrow. I want to spend some extra time with you."

My jaw dropped. I'd never called in since day one of my program. I had no need to.

"Call in and say what?" I asked.

"Figure it out. But I like this talking we're doing. I want to do more of it," he said.

I stared at him, perhaps looking as baffled as I felt. *What planet did this beautiful alien fall from?* Never had a man been so emotionally honest with me. On top of that, his finger was a thing of magic. The titillating sensation from his stimulation was working its way down between my legs.

I took a centering breath. "And you'll be honest with me if I sacrifice my professional image and perfect attendance record to spend the day with you?"

He chuckled. "That's a lot of sacrifice."

I pointed at him playfully. "Answer the question, Doctor."

His hand curved around my back, and he drew me to him.

"I'll be as honest as I possibly can," he said before planting a sensual kiss on me.

My pussy yearned for more of him as we rolled across the mattress, kissing and caressing, unable to get close enough or satiate our desire for each other. While we were still making out, he reached over and plucked another condom from the nightstand. I was so soaking wet down there that I could feel the moisture glazing my inner thighs. I watched him slide the rubber over his perfect dick. I could hardly believe I had scored in the fashion that I had. Not only was he hot, but he also had the kind of dick most men should envy.

Then Dr. Sparrow rolled on top of me. His

magnificent girth filled me. I gasped and held on tight as his swollen cock dove deep into me then glided out before plunging back into my depths.

I thrust my head against the pillow, clenching my back teeth as the nerves under my mound began to spark. Dr. Sparrow moaned as if he was feeling pleasure unheard of. I closed my eyes and raised my pelvis, chasing another intravaginal orgasm. I could hardly believe that he was capable of giving me one every time we made love. *What man can do that?* Jake Sparrow, that was who.

His dick kept plunging in and out of me so indulgently and deliciously.

Then it happened. "Ah…" I cried out as an orgasm built, one sensation after the next. "Oh!" My fingers dug into his skin. "Ah!" I convulsed while climaxing like I never had before.

Then Dr. Sparrow wrapped his arms around my thighs and pumped in and out of me like an oil derrick. That look of pure pleasure never left his face. Then like the last time he'd come, he grunted indulgently and sucked my neck until his orgasm had ended.

We remained in that position, our bodies rising and falling against each other as we breathed, dizzied by the warmth of being alive. His heaviness made me feel possessed by him. Where our sexual encounters would lead, neither of us knew, but they would not end, not any time soon, at least.

CHAPTER FIFTEEN

PENINA ROSS

The best time to call Deb was while I was totally exhausted and reeling from post-sex hormones. Deb was a stickler for making residents who had the flu stay home, so when I called in, I articulated the symptoms of having the virus without outright saying I had it.

"Then you'd better stay home and manage your health. By the way, I heard about your building. Where are you staying?"

My chest tightened. *Damn, I have to lie.* "At the W."

"The W Hotel?"

"Yes." I sounded strained.

"Are any of your cohorts in the room with you?" she asked.

"No. Only me."

"Good. I don't want you infecting anyone else. All we need is for flu to move through our department. We're already short-staffed as it is."

"True, we're very short-staffed. But I'll check in with you tomorrow evening and give you an update on my health," I said.

She said, "Okay," and that was that. I had done it. For the first time since my career as a resident started, I had called in sick.

Dr. Sparrow had been listening to my call. "Do you find that to be an impediment?" he asked.

I sat on the edge of the bed, hating the fact that I'd chosen to lie to my boss and trying to process his question.

"Do I find what to be an impediment?" I asked.

"The shortage of doctors and nurses."

My limbs felt heavy as I stood. "Of course. I mean, I had two very crucial surgeries yesterday, back-to-back. I'm a late-year resident, but I've technically been working as an attending for the past two years. However…" I raised a finger pointedly. "This is not me complaining about the last part of that." I managed a smile.

Dr. Sparrow walked over to wrap his arms

around me. Our lips merged, and we kissed in our usual sensual way.

"Mmm," he said as if my bitter mouth tasted like a butter cookie. "Go take a shower so you can get some sleep."

I sniffed gently. "No sleep for you, I presume."

"We'll see," he said. "I'll try."

One final kiss, and I trekked off to wash myself in his shower since it was my favorite. We also agreed to move my things to his room since as long as we were staying in his friend's penthouse, we would be making love and getting to know each other better.

I SHOWERED AND FINALLY BRUSHED MY TEETH. WHEN I was ready to go to bed, Dr. Sparrow was already between the sheets, naked and waiting for me.

Once I slid under the linens and was close enough, he seized me. His cock wasn't fully erect, but I gasped when it slid inside my weeping pussy from behind me.

I released a silken sigh. His manhood really knew how to make an impact.

"Your skin is soft, Penina," he whispered in my

ear. "Like a delicate rose." In and out, slow and deep, his shaft shifted through my moisture.

I wanted to whisper, "Thank you," but sheer enjoyment had rendered me speechless.

"I promise you that I'm trustworthy," he said and delicately bit my earlobe then reached around my waist to smash his fingers on my clit.

After that, I was slain.

My eyes opened slowly. I'd climaxed before I drifted off to sleep, and so had Jake. I wasn't sure if he'd fallen asleep, but I hoped so. However, once again, I woke up alone. So many mornings, I'd awakened alone, but for some reason, I hated the feeling of Jake not being there.

I found a fresh robe in his closet, and before I walked out of it, I spotted several dresses hanging on the bar. My heart sank to my stomach, but then I remembered he'd said I could trust him, and his friend was like family. Even if the friend was a woman, they were too close to be lovers. If the friend was a man, then the dresses could belong to the man's wife or girlfriend. Arriving at that conclusion allowed me to relax.

When I walked out of the room and to the kitchen to see if Jake had brunch prepared for me, I faintly heard his voice. He was home. I followed the sound and discovered him in a home office on the opposite side of the elevator. It was the first time I'd seen the room. And Jake looked so sexy sitting behind the desk. He had just set his cellphone down and stopped on his way to typing on the keyboard of his MacBook Pro.

"Hello," I said, beaming and waving by wiggling my fingers.

"Come here," he said, tilting his head.

My pulse raced as I strolled across the marble floor. I was surprised by how I was walking. I'd never fuck-walked to arouse a man in my life. I used to criticize those girls, but there I was, doing it myself.

When I was close enough, he seized me and slid a finger into my slit. I loved that it didn't take him more than one try to find my clit.

"How did you sleep?" he asked, his finger-work stimulating me.

My eyes flitted closed as the orgasmic sensation feathered through my pussy.

"Fine," I said breathlessly.

"I like the way this feels on my tongue," he whispered thickly.

I felt like guiding my hips more toward his stimulation, but my legs were getting weaker by the moment, making it hard to stand. Finally, he stopped and shoved his computer forward and his chair back.

"Sit on the desk," he ordered.

I did what he told me to do.

"Brace yourself," he said.

I could sort of figure out the positions we were about to take, so I pressed my palms on top of his desk. Jake rolled his chair toward me. The anticipation alone made me cream. Then he grasped my hips, and I nearly hyperventilated in the moments before his hot wet tongue laved my clit, then all of a sudden, the sensation he aroused went from three to ten.

I gasped loudly and continuously. I wanted to reach for his head to help him give me a little reprieve, but if I took my hands off the desk, I would fall backward. Sucking air like a fish out of water, I wondered how the hell he was doing that. My pussy was clamped against Jake's mouth, so I couldn't see how his tongue was making me lose my mind.

"Ah!" I cried as an orgasm streaked through my pussy.

He didn't stop. He made me scream repeatedly until my lower half felt exhausted. I was surprised how fast he could make my pussy ready for another orgasm. Eight times, I had come, and I thought he was ready to stop, but he wasn't. Jake kept his eyes on me, watching me writhe and cry and moan his name. After my last orgasm, he shot to his feet, unzipped his pants and crammed his rigid cock into me.

He fucked me hard, gritting his teeth, shouting, "Ha!" with each stab.

"Your…" Jab.

"Fucking…" Jab.

"Pussy…" Jab.

"Oh!" He pulled his dick out, and his warm milk sprayed all over my belly.

"Holy shit," I said. That was intense.

He slammed his palms on top of the desk, tonguing me like there was no tomorrow. "Are you on the pill?" he whispered thickly.

I shook my head, consumed by all facets of desire.

"We have to get you on the pill."

"No, I have an IUD," I whispered.

He frowned. "Why didn't you tell me? I could've saved myself the fucking condoms."

I couldn't believe we were having that conversation with his sperm on my stomach and my pussy on display. "Dr. Sparrow—"

"Why do you keep referring to me as Dr. Sparrow?" he asked.

"Because you're my superior."

His lopsided grin was sexy. "You taste good, and call me…"

I waited for him to officially give me permission to refer to him by his first name. Instead, he paused and watched me with a conflicted expression.

I cocked my head. "Call you…"

"Jake."

By the look that was on his face, I wasn't sure if he meant what he said or not, but since referring to him as Dr. Sparrow made me feel as if we were making no progress in the way of becoming closer, I decided that for private times and especially during sex, I would from that point onward refer to him as Jake.

CHAPTER SIXTEEN

PENINA ROSS

We cleaned ourselves then went into the dining room to have a late dinner. Jake ordered Louisiana-rub prime rib with lots of truffle fries per my request. I had just bitten down on my first French fry when he brought up the no-condom thing again.

"Come on, Jake, you know what I'm protecting myself from."

His sexy lopsided smile came back. "You don't have to protect yourself from me. I'm clean."

Damn, the fries were delicious. "Anyone can say they're clean." I shoved another into my mouth.

He licked his bottom lip. "I'm clean. Trust me. No STDs. I want to feel your heat and your wetness unobstructed."

I coughed because I almost choked. Damn, that made my pussy flex.

"Drink some water, Penina," he said.

I grabbed my glass and took a few gulps of it. I cleared my throat a few times then said, "My ex used to try to talk me out of using a condom. He always had itchy dick."

"Are you referring to Nurse Peters's partner?"

He sounded so formal, which made me want to laugh and fuck him bare. "Yes. I'm referring to Nurse Peters's partner," I replied, grinning.

"I assure you, he and I have nothing in common."

I felt my eyes smolder. "So far, you're showing me that, especially in the sack."

He let out a loud laugh, which I found fascinating. *Have I ever heard Jake laugh that way?* I didn't think so.

"Penina," he said, suddenly speaking with control again. And that same seductive way in which he spoke my name also made me horny.

"Yes, Jake?" I said breathlessly.

"We'll cross that road when we get to it?"

"What road?" I asked.

"Me fucking you bare?"

I tilted my head curiously. "Is that what we do?

Fuck? It feels like making love to me." I couldn't believe I'd said that.

He nodded. "I make love to you." He looked off.

When he faced me again, we stared at each other. Our exchange was quick but powerful.

Suddenly, he adjusted in his seat. "Can I ask you something?"

When I nodded, my head felt as though it was bobbing all over the place.

"Why did you choose this program? I saw your academic records. You could've gone to any of the top hospitals in the country. Why New Orleans?"

Something that felt a lot like love flooded my heart as I thought about the city. "New Orleans is my..." I hummed as I pondered the right word to call her. "My mistress."

He raised his eyebrows. "Humph. How so?"

I told him all about how I was first introduced to the city in college. Back then, I had so much fun dancing, eating, and falling in and out of love with boys over the weekends.

"This place is pure bliss, and there's always something going on. A parade. A festival. Fun can pop up at any moment, on any corner. But..." I sighed exasperatedly. "I haven't been able to partake in any of it since I started my program. So the city's like a mistress I've been keeping in a box, waiting to make love to her one day, and hopefully sooner rather than later."

He watched me as if he was mesmerized while stroking his chin. "Interesting."

My face felt warm. "I know, it's stupid." I'd never told anyone that before.

"No, it's not stupid. It's actually sexy—like you."

Remember to breathe, Pen, I repeated, staring into his fiery eyes.

To cool off, I plopped a few more truffle fries into my mouth. The flavor was divine.

"What about you? Although you'll never let me scrub in with you, I heard your techniques and efficiency in the OR are sheer perfection."

I expected him to smile smugly, but he didn't. Instead, Jake frowned. "I'll let you scrub in with me. But you're our finest resident. That's why Nordoff, Hyung, and Nassim are quick to sign off on your solos. They say that you don't fuck up."

"Yeah, but I've been working with those guys for seven years. They've taught me everything they know. You're new. It's time I learned from you."

He winked. "Point taken, Dr. Ross, and I'll see you in the OR on your next shift."

"I have a question for you," I said.

He raised his eyebrows, showing me an open expression.

"Why are you so indulgent in bed?"

He jerked his head back. "Indulgent?"

"It's like you're feeling sex between us down to your soul. I feel as if when you're making love to me, you're really in love with me." It was so my style to say something like that to a man with no regret.

He grunted thoughtfully. "I can easily fall in love with you. That's if you'll let me. But I…" Once again, he looked off with a frown. "I have a friend who has suffered a lot of abuse at the hands of men. It's because of her experiences that I want to do more than fuck a woman." He looked at me again. His expression beamed, then he cleared his throat and swallowed. "I was experiencing your body with your soul, and it was…" He sniffed, smirked, then bunched his fingers together and kissed the tips.

I could feel my smile stretching from one side of my face to the other.

"Likewise" came dripping out of my mouth like silky sweet honey. *Holy shit, I'm flirting.* That was new.

As two surgeons would, we ended up talking shop. He shared some of his methods with me and told me about his time as a resident in Australia. At one point, I felt as if I should grab a pen and paper and take some notes. He was smart, and I also noted that he fused principles of chemistry with biology. I liked Jake Sparrow. I could definitely let myself fall in love with him.

He was explaining the Winslow technique of separating the dura mater from the brain and draining excess fluid when he abruptly shook his finger.

"Tomorrow night," he said.

I threw my hands up excitedly. "I'm in. I'm all for learning the Winslow technique tomorrow night. Late surgery, though, right?"

He smirked. "Such an eager surgeon. You're in the right field, Dr. Ross." He leaned toward me. "But that's not it. Tomorrow night, we're going to fuck your mistress."

I furrowed my brow. "My..." Then I slapped myself on the forehead and said, "Oh."

He chuckled as his cellphone beeped, and I was familiar with the sound. He frowned as he read a message. "Shit, I have to go to the hospital."

"Oh," I said, intrigued by the possibility of scrubbing in with him as soon as in a few hours."

He winked at me as he stood. "No, beautiful, you stay here. You're catching the flu, remember? You're also going to need another day off."

I sank in my seat as if all the air had been drained out of me. Listening to him go on about his experience and techniques made me eager to see him in action.

"By the way," he said.

I straightened my face, erasing the frown. "What?" I sounded hopeful.

"Let's do something more like fucking before I go."

I tossed my head back and laughed. Then I made firm eye contact with him. "Yes. Let's."

CHAPTER SEVENTEEN

PENINA ROSS

I lay in bed with my hands behind my head. With a cock with the girth of Jake's, I had experienced the most effective quickie in the history of quickies. We both came in a matter of minutes. He instructed me to keep eating and relaxing as much as I could. Tomorrow night, we would be out late, but he swore we would have a lot of fun.

"What are we going to do?" I asked, excitedly watching him put on clothes.

It felt different between us. It was as if that asshole I'd first met smoking in front of our building never existed. Perhaps because I knew he was behaving that way because he was attracted to me. Jake was a thinker. Never in a million years had I thought I would be involved with a man who thought a whole lot before he acted.

"I can't say," he said then slipped on his shirt.

It was a shame to no longer see his ripped chest.

"Do you go to the gym?" I asked.

He smirked. "Every day. When I can't sleep, I work out, and I've now added making love to my exercise program."

My cheeks heated as he smirked at me.

Then we engaged in a long, luscious, passionate, pulse-pounding kiss. When Jake held me, it was as if his hands and body took complete possession of my entire being.

My head felt dizzy as I watched him walk away from me. I lay on the bed and listened to him rushing through the penthouse for a few minutes, then the elevator dinged. He was gone.

Wasting no time following the doctor's orders, I drew a warm bath in the claw-foot tub in the master bathroom. As I laid my head back against the ceramic, I recalled every one of our lovemaking sessions. Boy, was he good at sex. *How did he learn to go down on a woman that way?*

Unfortunately, my mind also replayed instances when Rich had laved me up down there as he tried to find the clit. It was a gross, sloshy saliva bath. At least he gave me more moisture to swallow his long cock. But with all the women he cheated with, not one of us was able to teach him how to stimulate the clit.

Then I remembered that Rich wasn't such a great student. I even gave him a touch-the-clit example once, but he merely snatched his hand out of my grasp and said, "I don't need a lesson on eating pussy. I know how to eat pussy."

I was too kind to insult him and say, *Dude, if you knew how to do it, then I wouldn't be giving you a lesson. Do you think I want to be doing this?*

Squeezing my eyes even tighter, I once again banished my ex from my mind. I had no idea why I thought about him so much lately. I didn't love him. Perhaps it was because, as boyfriends went, he was the extreme example of my picker being off.

I slid my finger down my slit, recalling Jake's desk and my being on top of it and his mouth pleasuring me. I so hoped my picker was working when it came to him.

He's hiding something, a small voice whispered inside my head.

My eyes popped open, and my chest felt heavy. I would have to accept that he was indeed keeping secrets. I also had to remember that I loved his company and making love to him. What I couldn't do was fall in love with him, not until I knew everything he was hiding.

I settled on taking that position, which allowed me to relax more in the warm water. I washed myself with a gardenia-and-citrus body scrub then went into the shower to rinse off the delicious-smelling granules. After I was done washing and blow-drying my hair, I ordered dessert, an assortment of fried donuts with delicious dipping sauces.

My stomach was so full after I devoured dessert that I clutched it as I walked to the master bedroom to lie down for a bit. But as I passed the door of the guest room, I heard my cellphone ding with a text message.

"Damn it," I muttered, realizing I should've had it with me in Jake's room. Even though I was off shift, I still had to be reachable.

I sat on the foot of the bed and checked my messages. Of course, my team had plenty of questions about patients. I raced to my computer and powered it on. I decided to work in the office. I was sure Jake wouldn't mind.

"Jake." I said his name as I waited for my computer finishing booting. "Jake," I said again.

Gosh, how easily his name formed in my mouth.

I hated that I felt he was the one. He couldn't be the one.

"The secrets, Pen," I whispered.

Once my desktop appeared, I answered all the emails regarding patients I had passed off. Then I saw that one email that made my chest contract. I rubbed my breastbone as I looked at the first few lines of the message from Boston in the previewer. It read, "Congratulations, Dr. Penina Ross."

"Shit," I said under my breath.

I had been accepted.

When a loud ding announced another message, I jumped. It was from Angela.

I smell you on him. And you know who I'm talking about.

I gasped sharply then slapped my hand over my mouth. I'd forgotten to warn him about Angela's bearlike sense of smell. There was no way of hiding it from her. I had to trust that she would keep her discovery to herself.

I sat for a while, wondering how to respond. But the best response was no response. I closed my laptop, and since I was practicing avoidance, I put Boston out of my mind too. I went to the bed where Jake and I last made love, wrapped myself in the blankets, which smelled like the both of us, and went to sleep.

"PEN," SOMEONE SAID SOFTLY.

I opened my eyes slowly. Jake was beside me. His shirt was off, and it looked as if he had been beside me for a while.

"Hey," I said tiredly. "What time is it?"

"It's six a.m. I have to go into surgery."

My head felt fuzzy, and it was hard to process what he had said. "But you just got out of surgery."

"I've been here next to you for a while." He started nibbling my neck, and I knew why he'd woken me.

Jake took off his night pants as we were kissing. *It's six a.m.? Right.* I was off that day.

I sighed as his cock dove into my pussy.

WHEN I WOKE UP AGAIN, THE CURTAINS WERE OPEN, but the sheer shades covered the glass. The scent of lemon cleanser hung in the air. I had learned that was a sign the maids had been cleaning.

I struggled to shift into a sitting position. I was still drowsy but also well rested, which was something my body hadn't felt in many, many years.

Six a.m. this morning... Jake was here. We made love.

His body felt so strong on top of me. I squeezed my thighs together, and a thrill sparked through my pussy. His dick made me so sensitive down there. His sensual way of making love caused me to crave him every waking hour.

"That's right," I said and sighed, remembering that Angela knew we were having sex. I would confirm her findings the next time we saw each other, but until then, I would make her wait.

As usual, breakfast was set up in the kitchen. That time, the flowers were two dozen red roses. I took a while to smell each one of them before diving into a full-on feast with all the trimmings—scrambled eggs, hash browns, crepes, breakfast meats, an array of fruit, and a variety of breads. I wasn't used to eating as much as I had since staying in the penthouse, and I was positive I'd gained a couple of pounds—love pounds, which was the best kind of weight to pile on. Regardless, I decided to take it easy and put a serving of eggs, an English muffin, and turkey bacon on my plate.

While I ate and drank coffee, I did something I

hadn't done in a long time. I turned on the television just in time to see news coverage about a guy running for a Senate seat in California, my home state. They ran a clip of his performance on New Day America, which happened a week ago. The host, Tia Rose, notorious for emotional theatrics, had gotten the guy, whose name was Spencer Christmas, to talk about his wife in a favorable way.

"Christmas," I whispered. I felt as though someone had mentioned that name to me recently, but I couldn't remember who.

The guy's wife was the daughter of Patricia Forte, whom I'd voted for twice. One somber-looking dude in the studio argued with a woman who looked more like a naughty librarian than a journalist, if that was what she was supposed to be. He said Spencer Christmas could've beat Patricia Forte. She said Spencer Christmas was smart to drop out of the race this weekend because he hadn't stood for anything other than being a billionaire who knew how to give away money.

I rubbed the side of my face. *Has another weekend gone by without me realizing it?* I closed my eyes and remembered that it was Tuesday.

"Talk about money, she still has an ongoing corruption case—campaign finance fraud."

My eyes grew wide. *Wow, I didn't know that.*

"That has been proven false, Byron. I can't believe of all people, you were never willing to test this guy."

"I have tested him. Sure, he's a Washington outsider, but what his foundation has done for victims of his father's crimes speaks for itself. Plus, he's young. Every senator has to start somewhere, or else they would've been in Congress for too long. Kind of like Forte."

She grunted as if he'd just slapped her in the face then started using her fingers to count down. "He's never held an office in his life. He's a playboy."

"That's not fair," Byron said. "The guy's faithfully married."

"Listen," the somber guy, who was clearly the referee, said. "This is an example of how polarizing this contest was and still is. None of us thought Forte would go down without a fight, but she pulled out. Mike Black is our new frontrunner. Does he have the juice to go all the way?"

I turned the channel when the woman groaned and rolled her eyes. That entire situation was giving me a headache. Instead, I stopped on a show about ancient apothecary. I couldn't believe my luck. I got comfortable on the big mustard-colored suede sectional sofa.

Then the doorbell chimed.

"Damn it," I said, springing to my feet.

I pressed pause on the remote control, and the video stopped. I pumped my fist. "Yes." I wouldn't miss any of the program.

"Dr. Ross," came a voice over the PA system. "I have a delivery for you from Jake."

When I opened the door, a man wearing a suit and carrying a large white box came inside and said he had been told to take the box to the bedroom, and I was not to open it. He made me promise I would not look inside.

I raised my right hand. "I will not."

The guy smiled. "I'll impart your answer to Dr. Sparrow."

Of course, I cheesed like a Cheshire cat as I closed the door behind me. It felt sexy to know that he would be relaying my answer to Jake.

Once it was just the box and me in the penthouse, I jogged to the bedroom and stared at it. Jake had said that we were going out to bang my mistress that night. *Did he buy me a dress?* Of course he had. All my party clothes were at my apartment. I so very much wanted to see what he'd picked out. I wondered if he could figure out my taste. I wasn't the sort of woman who sat my sexuality on the table for all the men to sniff around. I liked elegance—sophistication mixed with contemporary style. For instance, I would wear a low-back cocktail dress with one spaghetti-strap. Jake couldn't know that about me with the little time we'd spent together. We would have to spend more time in each other's lives. He would have to become my boyfriend.

I counted the days in my head. Wow, we had known each other for sixteen days.

CHAPTER EIGHTEEN

PENINA ROSS

I had so much anxiety that I didn't know what to do with myself. I'd never been away from the hospital for that long, so I didn't know if my angst was from that or being so curious to find out what was in that box. I had to do something and get moving. But I didn't want to run the risk of running into someone I knew by going back to my apartment and getting my workout clothes. I was pretty sure the luxury building had a phenomenal gym. I needed to take a one hour walk on a treadmill or something. Then I remembered that I suspected Jake's friend might be a woman since I'd seen dresses in the closet, and she had to have other clothes in some of the drawers, including workout gear.

I searched through a credenza with a beautiful

wood pattern in the front and scored. Yoga pants, a T-shirt, and a few bikinis were inside.

I was pretty sure Jake wouldn't mind if I wore them. We both knew how important even the lowest-impact exercise was for the body. Plus, he had encouraged me to make myself at home more than once.

If I were at home and twiddling my thumbs on an afternoon when my brain was used to being in surgery or consults or troubleshooting the best way to get at a clot or a tumor, I would go to Bellies to see who I could run into and strike up a conversation. But I couldn't do that because I was supposed to be monitoring myself for symptoms of the flu. Another thing I would do was read what was new in *Neuro Journal Today,* which usually took me away for hours at a time. But I was too excited about the dress box and my tryst with Dr. Jake Sparrow to concentrate on reading. Therefore, I chose to exercise.

I put on the woman's clothes, which fit me a little snugly. The person they belonged to had to be at least fifteen to twenty pounds lighter than me. Next, I called the front desk to ask on which floor I would find the gym. They told me to take the elevator down two floors and put my finger on the door pad, and I should be granted entrance. I followed the directions precisely, and soon I was on the treadmill at the beginning of a brisk walk.

The gym was empty, which was sort of a letdown. It would've been nice to start a conversation with someone who lived in the building and figure out if they knew anything about the owners of the penthouse. Regardless, I was thirty minutes into my exercise, and my breathing was good, and my legs were strong. At the one-hour mark, I'd walked over three and a half miles. My feet were hurting because I had on the wrong shoes, but my lungs felt reinvigorated.

I took my shoes off and hobbled all the way back to the elevator, thinking that I'd messed up. Jake wanted to take me out that night. I would never be able to comfortably wear a pair of heels.

"Heels!" I gasped as I entered the elevator to return to the penthouse. I had no shoes to wear with that dress.

But then I calmed myself again. I was certain Jake had all the bases covered.

I TOOK A LONG BATH POST-WORKOUT. THAT TIME, AS I soaked in the warm water, I had no thoughts weighing me down. Also, my feet felt a lot better. I promised to never exercise in the wrong shoes again. But the walk had worked. I was in a total restful state when the doorbell rang.

"Damn it," I whispered, head still resting on the lip of the tub without moving an inch. I was considering waiting it out until they went away.

"Dr. Ross, we're here to prepare you for the evening," a woman said through the PA.

Excitement made me get out of the tub as fast as I could. I had to be careful, though. Water was dangerous. One slip, and whatever Jake had planned for us would be over.

I dried myself with a bath towel, slid on a robe and slippers, and shuffled to the door.

THE TEAM WHO ARRIVED AT MY DOOR PROVED JUST how much of a fashionista or glamour girl I wasn't. I liked my face to look dewy and fresh whenever I dressed up to go out and have a good time. That meant a little red, plum, or pink lipstick, mascara, light eyeliner, and a sweep of blush over translucent power. It always seemed to get the job done. However, two makeup artists, a hairdresser, and a stylist made me look unrecognizable within two hours.

I studied my reflection in the standing mirror. My dress was a long silver slip gown that caressed my curves like an erotic kiss. According to Desiree, the stylist, the straps of my dress were made of pure diamonds, and so were the stones on my strappy sandals. Vivian, the hairdresser, had managed to whip my usually wayward hair into an array of big and loose cascading ringlets. I wore an exquisite cat mask, which covered half my face. It was ornately encrusted with gold, pearls, and diamonds. The thing must've cost more money than I could fathom ever making in a lifetime. Purchasing the penthouse for a friend then having so much disposable cash to woo me in a major way, Jake must've had a huge bank account.

After all the loose ends were tied, the crew bowed out of the apartment and said they would send someone back the next day to collect the goods. When I took it all off, I was to lay each item carefully across the chair in Jake's room. I said goodbye to them, and just like that, I was alone in the apartment, dressed like a wealthy, sexy, and pampered cat.

"What next?" I muttered.

Right on cue, the house phone rang, and I carefully padded over to answer it.

"Take the elevator to P-1. I'm waiting for you," Jake said then hung up before I could ask him where we were going.

What was happening was so far out of the ordinary that I had to take a moment to keep myself from panicking. "One step at a time, Pen," I whispered.

My heart raced a mile a minute when I stepped into the elevator. Nerves made me light-headed as I pressed the P-1 button.

On the way down, I studied myself in the gold-paneled walls. I looked as if I belonged in one of those commercials for a chichi hotel in Las Vegas, suggesting I was on my way out to indulge in an activity that was naughty, furtive, and out of this world.

The doors slid open, and a few steps away sat a sleek black limousine with tinted windows. The back door opened, and Jake stepped out of the back seat. My eyes grew wide, and I inhaled sharply. He wore a black suit that made him look like a sexy James Bond and a soft black cotton shirt beneath the jacket. He also had on a golden mask encrusted with onyx and diamonds and fashioned in the shape of a wolf. His appearance was just as expensive as mine was.

Finally, we were face-to-face. After trailing the back of his fingers down the side of my face, Jake curled an arm around my waist and drew me against his hard body.

"There are no words to describe how you look." His voice was fueled by passion.

Jake ran his hands down my bare shoulders as his lips gently pressed against mine. Our tongues connected, brushing delicately. The way we were making out sent my head floating to the sky.

"The cat and the wolf," I whispered when we moved our lips apart to take a breath.

Jake chuckled then kissed me again. Something told me that we would be doing a lot of smooching throughout the evening.

A WINDOW SEPARATED THE BACK SEAT OF THE LIMO from the front, so it felt as if Jake and I were in our own universe. It had been a while since I'd ventured off to admire the mansions in the Garden District of New Orleans. I used to visit the neighborhood often when I was an intern. There used to be days I couldn't fall asleep after my shift ended to save my life. Exams, surgical procedures, and material from the day's symposium cluttered my mind. Walking through that neighborhood helped me battle my insomnia. I would stop in front of my favorite properties and stare at the decorative wrought iron gates, the barrier between me and the lush lawns, manicured trees, and white stone mansions with their colossal columns and wrap-around balconies. Even though many of the French colonial manors were being remodeled, I could still envision a lady of the house resting on a red velvet chaise lounge in the cool of the day, full of pampered self-absorption.

That was why it felt so odd that two neurosurgeons who considered discussing surgical techniques foreplay were in a limousine and dressed for a party rooted in fifteenth-century Italy. I had to convince myself that swallowing a bite of Medici family lavishness and Southern extravagance wasn't too ridiculous.

"This is a lot," I whispered.

He dipped his tongue into my mouth and kissed me again. Then Jake's teeth delicately captured my lower lip as he slid his tongue across it. "You deserve more," he replied breathlessly.

I wondered why he thought so as I gently sucked my bottom lip into my mouth to taste him.

"You're frowning," he said, his brow furrowed.

"It's just…" I sighed. I didn't want to overthink it or be a Debbie Downer.

"You don't believe you deserve more?" he asked.

"No more than anyone else," I replied, happy to get that off my chest.

"To me, you deserve the world," he said, gazing into my eyes.

I tilted my head and narrowed my eyes suspiciously. "You speak like a man with a lot of money. Are you a man with a lot of money, Jake Sparrow?"

He chortled as he smirked. "I spend where I find it necessary."

Oh, that was smooth. And the fact that I was so captivated by his gaze made me not want to call him on it.

I asked him how his surgeries had gone, and he said that they went well. He'd almost lost a patient, but the person on his operating table fought like hell to stay with us. But any conversation about work couldn't last long on such a night. I put a hand on his strong chest, and his lips found mine.

I wanted to know if he was as aroused as I was, so I let my hand slide down his abs and gently caress his dick. Damn, he was as solid as a steel pipe.

Something flashed in his eyes as I shifted my hand up and down his shaft. He took in a deep breath through his nostrils before putting his hand on top of mine.

"Later, baby. I don't want to cut our night short." His voice was made thick by lust.

I wiggled my eyebrows, peering at him suggestively. "I'm always game for turning the car around and spending the rest of the evening in bed with you."

He shook his head. "I want to dance with you tonight," he said then kissed me softly. "Even though…" He took a gentle breath. "That offer is so fucking hard to refuse. I've been thinking about you all day long. And whenever I look at you, my neurons tell my body that I must have you. That's never happened to me before."

"Have you ever been in love?" I had never been in love, yet I felt the same way he did.

His brow pulled into an intense frown. "Once."

I gulped, instantly feeling a pinch of jealousy. It was silly, but I felt it regardless. "With whom?"

"A woman who was in love with my brother."

I tried to control the way my eyes wanted to

dance. He had just revealed something personal to me, and I didn't want him to realize it and go back to being overly secretive. Instead, I smiled flirtatiously. "Then I'm the second woman your neurons have reacted to."

"No," he said immediately. "I didn't feel the same for her. My love for her was not sexual or romantic. It was born from…"

I hung on to his every word, but it seemed as if he was struggling to continue whatever he was thinking.

"Born from?" I asked, gently encouraging him to speak what was on his mind.

The limousine came to a stop.

"Born from nothing good," he finally said.

"Did your brother care that you were in love with her?"

He sniffed. "No, he didn't. He didn't love her, so he wouldn't have cared." Jake shifted abruptly in his seat. "We should go inside."

With that one statement, the heaviness dissolved out of the air. I broke eye contact to turn and see what was behind me. A traditional Southern colonial mansion sat behind the lush lawn and trees, which canopied over a sidewalk that had warm orange lights running along each side of it. A restless feeling raced through me. I wanted to stay in the car and get to the bottom of Jake's neurons and learn more about his brother and his ex-girlfriend. But I also wanted to discover what was inside that mansion.

"This place looks seductive. That's for sure," I whispered.

As soon as I turned to face Jake, his mouth covered mine. He kissed me so fervently that he guided my back down onto the seat. Then I felt a jolt as our masks collided.

"Fuck," Jake said, rubbing his mask at the spot that covered his forehead. "Are you okay?"

I chuckled. "I'm fine. But we should do either-or—make out until we can't stop ourselves from going to the next step"—I wiggled my brows—"or go inside and discover what kind of excitement awaits us." Both options would've been equally pleasurable.

"Let's go," Jake said then helped me into a sitting position. Without pause, he got out of the limo and opened my door.

Taking his hand, I squinted at the unlit windows of the sprawling mansion. "Are we the only ones here?"

Jake winked. "We'll have to see, won't we?"

We walked side by side up the path. My nerves made me hold his hand tightly, and he let go of it to put his arm around me. I loved that he did that. The gesture made me feel safe and secure, even though I was still shaking a little as we ventured up the steps that led to the grand porch.

Jake let go of me to lift the lid over a keypad pasted against the stucco.

"Is this your mansion?" I asked.

Jake put his arm around me again. "No," he said as he pushed the door open.

I pressed a hand against my jumpy heart as we stepped into a large, dimly lit vestibule that ran from one end of the manor to the other. I wrinkled my nose because I could smell fresh plaster and paint. About two feet ahead of us was another door.

"This almost feels like *Alice in Wonderland*," I remarked.

Jake smirked as he pressed his balled fist against the wood. "Are you ready?"

My smile was pensive.

"Relax, beautiful. This is all fun," he said.

I nodded stiffly.

Then he knocked three times, and the door opened by itself.

CHAPTER NINETEEN

PENINA ROSS

It was thrilling. Jake, countless others, and I were in a grand ballroom. The hardwood floors were suitable for dancing under all the glittering chandeliers hanging from the high ceiling. The atmosphere was still dim, only decorated by sconces casting warm light. Masked men and women danced, drank, and had lively interactions with each other. So much stimulation was in the atmosphere that my brain couldn't focus on one thing at a time. A brass band was positioned on a platform. Each member wore a black-tie suit and a mask that resembled that of the main character from *The Phantom of the Opera*.

Jake led me to the space where everyone was dancing. "Tonight we're having a threesome with your mistress," he said with his mouth close to my ear so that I could hear him.

My heart beat like a bass drum. I was terrified that my moves might be rusty. I hadn't shaken my ass on the dance floor since before medical school. Sure, I'd gone to parties with Rich, but I'd always been too exhausted to participate in the fun. Suddenly, I understood Rich's constant complaints when it came to going out with me. He used to say I would yawn the entire time, and he took it as my sending him a message that I was bored. At the moment, I felt better than I had in a long time. Absorbed by the electrical or neurological chemistry between me and Jake, once we were in position, my body felt free to do whatever the hell it wanted to do next.

First, we danced our own version of the Charleston, moving back and forth in perfect harmony with each other. He was great at it. Then he seized my hand and took me for a few spins. We laughed together. Then he drew me in for a kiss. His dick was hard. The music was faster than our pace. It was as though we were in a slow dance and our lust for each other was playing a passionate tune only he and I could hear.

At some point, the song changed, and Jake and I

went at it again. I shimmied my shoulders at him, gyrated my hips against his boner, then rubbed my ass against his man of steel.

When it got to be too much, he would fasten his hands on my hips, pull me against him, and whisper, "Slow down, baby."

I could hardly believe I was having such a good time in the city again. Jake and I were going in for our hundredth kiss or so when a masked woman nudged him on the shoulder.

"Hey, don't I know you?" she asked.

Jake peered at her, then she took off her mask.

"It's me, Renata," she said.

He watched her a few seconds longer then shook his head. "No. I don't know you."

The way his eyes widened just a fraction made me think he had indeed recognized her.

"Oh," she said, sounding shocked by his response. "It's just the way you carry yourself and your…" Her eyes narrowed to slits as her hand flew up and her fingers spread across her clavicle. "Really, you don't remember—"

"I don't know you, miss. Please excuse us."

Renata remained still as she watched him, baffled. "I'm sorry," she said finally. "I must've mistaken you for someone else."

I wanted so badly to ask, *Who else*? But I merely nodded at her as he guided me away from the scene and said something about getting us food and drink. He led me toward a decadent spread of hot cuisines and a fully serviced open bar.

"That was weird," I said after Jake ordered scotch on the rocks.

He pointed at me. "What will you have?" he asked.

I could tell he was shaken by his interaction with the woman, even though he was trying not to show it.

"Sparkling water with lime."

He nodded and ordered it for me.

As the bartender prepared our drinks, Jake seized my hand and kissed the back of it. He put his mouth close to my ear. "I didn't know you were such a hot dancer. It turns me on."

Then he kissed me. As our tongues laved each other and my body rose against him, all I could think about was that woman. Jake must've forgotten how perceptive I was. He indeed knew her, and I was determined to find out who she thought he was before our night at the mansion was over.

CHAPTER TWENTY

PENINA ROSS

Jake engaged me in a mission to taste a little of everything on the buffet, like the deconstructed shrimp po' boy, jambalaya rolls, red beans and rice, and crawfish etouffee. Gumbo shots were served in mini bread cups large enough for us to pour the contents into our mouths and enjoy chewing the one succulent shrimp, a plump piece of crab, and andouille sausage along with the buttery crusted bread that held the delicious surprise in only a few bites.

I knew I should've stopped at one, but I was on my sixth gumbo shot.

"Whoa," I said, savoring the flavors, which were still in my mouth after swallowing. "That was good.

How did you get an invitation to this party in the first place?"

"A friend," he said finally. By his tentative smirk, I could tell that the openness he'd had in the limousine was a thing of the past. That woman had certainly shaken him up.

I smiled warmly at him. "Well, tell your secret friend thank you."

He took a swig of the same cocktail he'd ordered earlier. Jake wasn't a big drinker, and I liked that about him.

Then he put his mouth near my ear. "When are you going to trust me?"

The answer was easy. I put my mouth close to his ear. "I trust you. But still, you're hiding a lot from me."

He moved his mouth back near my ear. "Like what?"

I switched positions with him again. "You tell me."

Jake leaned away from me to study me as if he could see my full expression past my mask. Suddenly, my stomach grumbled. I'd eaten too much and needed some relief.

I clamped a hand over my belly and said, "I'm going to the ladies' room. Think about your answer while I'm gone." I winked at him. Before I could leave him, Jake tugged me against him for another hot and heavy smooch. When our lips parted, I was dizzy and wobbly as I walked away.

THE PATH TO THE LADIES' ROOM WAS DOWN A LONG corridor where the walls were a long decorative iron screen with frosted glass behind it. Soft light lingered beyond the glass, and I immediately wanted to know what was behind the barrier. Also, the atmosphere was vaporous, and a mild perfume lingered in the air.

I didn't even notice the women standing in line to use the restroom until I came upon the last person. When I asked her, I learned that I wasn't the only one having problems digesting the tasty but rich gumbo shots, which were still rumbling in my stomach. I counted all the bodies standing in line.

"There are fourteen people ahead of us," I said.

The woman stole a glance at me. "There are six stalls, so it shouldn't be that long."

I thanked her. It was nice of her to take the sting out of waiting for me.

As I settled at the end of the line, a masked man

wearing a red suit with a ruffled white shirt appeared out of the vapors beyond the bathroom door and headed in our direction. I stood straighter when he stopped beside me.

"Ma'am, you're VIP. Please proceed upstairs to the VIP restroom."

My jaw dropped. *How in the world can he identify me as VIP?* My stomach grumbled again, so I chose not to question him about it.

"What stairs?" I asked.

"Continue up the hallway, and you'll find them."

The woman standing in front of me stole a glance at me, curiosity in her eyes. Whatever was in my stomach wanted out, so I nodded and started walking as fast as I could. When I reached the end of the corridor, there was only one way to turn. But instead of moving forward, I stopped in my tracks. The woman who'd questioned Jake earlier was right there.

I THOUGHT SHE WAS GOING TO WALK PAST ME without saying a word, and I was about to say, *Hi, Renata.*

However, Renata pressed a hand over her chest

and said, "I'm sorry for disturbing you and your partner earlier. I really thought I recognized him."

I looked deeper into her eyes. "I'm sorry. May I ask who you thought he was?"

She rubbed her elbow nervously. "Umm… just an old acquaintance I'd run into from time to time."

I tilted my head curiously. "An acquaintance? That's pretty casual."

She cracked a tiny smile. "Well… our circle is small but mighty."

I was thrown off a little by her bragging.

"But it's the way he carries himself. Like…." She shook her head as if it was difficult to come up with the words to explain it. My heart sank because I knew exactly how she felt. "Just… I'm sorry."

I imagined myself taking up all the space in the hallway and not allowing her to get past me. But she was talking, and that was good.

"Was his name Dr. Jake Sparrow?" I asked, sounding desperate for an answer.

"Doctor? No." She shook her head adamantly.

"What about Jake Sparrow?"

"No."

"Then who did you think he was?"

Suddenly, she directed her attention above my head.

Two large hands clamped down on my shoulders before I could turn around. I recognized his touch. Slowly, I faced him, and I stared into Dr. Jake Sparrow's eyes. I'd never seen such anger in them until then.

JAKE GAVE ME SPACE TO USE THE LADIES' ROOM, BUT AS soon as I was done, he led me out of the party. The limousine driver held the back door open for us. I slid into the back seat first, and he entered behind me. On the way back to the penthouse, unlike our ride to the masquerade party, Jake sat on one side of the car, and I sat on the other. As the car rolled along, he kept his eyes forward. I felt as though he was refusing to look at me.

I sighed hard to fill the aggressive silence.

"Why are you angry with me?" I blurted.

"I'm not angry," he said.

"You look angry. You feel angry, and distant."

Jake scratched the back of his neck. "I think we should cool it for a while."

My heart sank to my knees. "But why?" I couldn't believe I sounded so desperate. And he still hadn't looked at me yet.

"It'll be best that way."

I shook my head. "I don't understand. Why would it be best?"

"Because I'm your boss," he snapped.

I sniffed sarcastically. "You were my boss the first time you kissed me and fucked me."

His Adam's apple bobbed. "That's correct, which is why we should stop."

I could hardly believe what was happening. Before he'd caught me questioning the woman, we'd danced, laughed, kissed, and eaten well. We were falling in love with each other. *Does any of that matter anymore?*

"Jake?" My tone was stern.

His jaw tightened. "Yes, Penina?"

Still, the way he said my name set my heart on fire. "Look at me." He hadn't moved a muscle. "Please," I whispered.

Jake turned his head slowly. When our eyes met, I wondered if his pulse was pounding as hard as mine was. I also noticed how his harsh expression softened a bit before hardening again.

My mouth opened as I considered saying I was sorry. But I didn't think I was.

"Did you know who that woman was?" I asked.

His eyes narrowed to slits.

"I take your silence as a yes," I said.

"You can stay in the penthouse as long as needed, but we'll keep our distance," he said.

Suddenly, anger raced through me. Then tears flooded my eyes. My picker was still picking the wrong type of man to fall in love with. If everything was going his way, then we were in bliss. The moment something challenged his power and control, he was ready to walk out the door. *Fuck him.* I refused to let my tears fall.

I turned to gaze at my mistress beyond the window. She was so beautiful, so attractive when night fell upon her.

"Fine," I said, making my voice clear and unaffected.

I thought I could feel his eyes upon me, but I refused to look. I had to sleep at the penthouse that night, and in the morning, I would wake up and pull my shift. It was great that I had forgotten to call Deb and ask for another day off. The sooner I got back to life before Jake Sparrow, if that was even his real name, the better. After my shift ended and handoffs were complete, I would return to the penthouse, collect my things, and finally get a room at the W Hotel.

Through the reflections in the window, I could

see Jake watching me. But I wouldn't turn to watch him back. He hadn't said anything, and neither had I. We were done. My heart had been shattered into a million pieces.

THE DRIVE FELT AS THOUGH IT WENT BY IN A BLINK OF an eye. At some point, I'd taken my mask off, but I couldn't remember when. I couldn't even recall the movement I made two seconds ago. The car rolled slowly down the ramp and into the subterranean parking garage then stopped in front of the elevator. That was the first time I turned to look at Jake since he'd suggested we keep our distance. He was already watching me. I felt my breath slip heavily across my lips as we stared at each other. As soon as Jake ripped his eyes away from me, the driver hopped out of his seat and opened my door.

One of my feet touched the concrete. "You're not coming up?"

"No," Jake said, sounding strained.

I was sure my eyes conveyed the depths of my disappointment. Sadness pervaded my soul, and even if I searched, the right words weren't ready to come to me. My shoulders slumped as I got out of the vehicle and dragged myself to the elevator. The driver pushed the up button. I hadn't realized he was standing there. I thanked him by smiling at him faintly.

"Penina," Jake called.

I squeezed my eyes closed, braced myself, then opened them as I turned. His electric pale-blue eyes made me rub my palm over the heaviness in my chest.

Again, we stared at each other. I prayed he would jump out of the back seat, take me in his arms, and apologize for saying we needed some space. I was willing to forgive him. Then the elevator dinged as the doors slid open. Still, I waited for him to say something.

"Rest well, Penina," he said.

I pressed my lips into a grimace. Instead of waiting for him to roll up his window or order the driver to leave, I turned away first and entered the elevator. I forced myself to accept the fact that he and I were over as I studied the woman in the gold panels, wearing the beautiful dress. A sigh escaped me as I thought about all the ways Jake had touched me that night, his hard body against mine and his hands sliding up and down my hips or resting on my derrière or back. We were so intimate, our interaction so natural.

As the elevator opened to the penthouse floor, I talked myself into believing we were through. I had to, or else my anger would ignite me into a ball of fire. The lonely, hollow sounds of my footsteps moving down the marble-floored hallway helped convince me Jake and I were a thing of the past. With my arms crossed, shoulders slumped, I refused to cry. *I will not cry.*

CHAPTER TWENTY-ONE

JAKE SPARROW/ASHER CHRISTMAS

It took years to perfect the art of observation. One must sit still, barely breathing, and keep the eyes fastened on the object of one's desire. Penina slept in the bed. I had slept with several women—slept with, not fucked—and none of them appeared so restful as she. Her soul was at peace, and I wasn't sure if she knew that about herself.

What I had said to her earlier wouldn't disturb her rest. And I was glad she was getting plenty of it. We were surgeons, and that meant we lived in a perpetual state of fatigue. Before I met Penina, I'd savored the exhaustion. Fighting weakness in my body made me feel feeble, as if I kept one foot in the grave. Maybe that was the goal—to die as Jake Sparrow. But that had changed. I could smell my former life drawing nearer, getting ready to close in on me. I didn't want to be wiped off the face of the Earth anymore. I wanted to live happily ever after with her. What a fool I was to think I could put distance between us. *But here I am. What a fool.*

She snored, and I raised my chin to see if I could get a better look at her face. I couldn't catch a view of it, and that was disappointing, so I had to imagine the sexy and beautiful face of the woman who was slowly becoming everything I thought I never needed.

I had Kirk, my driver, drop me off at the Christmas family property on Third Street, and I used Bryn's security code to enter. Since the house hadn't been prepared for arrivals, it held stifling heat and humidity. There was no relief from its heaviness. It also felt as if the ghosts that haunted the hallways refused to scramble even after I turned on the lights. I wasn't frightened of anything tortured and non-human, though. I'd grown up in a house where evil spirits permeated every corner. As a child, I was afraid of them. They haunted my sleep and dashed across my ceiling, taking advantage of my vulnerability. When I was a teenager, I ignored them, and by adulthood, I knew they had no bite, no power beyond convincing humans they were mightier than what they were.

With a garment bag over one shoulder and a duffel over the other, I took off my mask and walked briskly. I hadn't planned on staying long. I went into one of the bedrooms, opened the duffel bag, took out a pair of black pants, a T-shirt, and a pair of sneakers and put them on. Then I hung my suit on the hangers in the garment bag.

Next, I walked the mask down to the darkest part of the house, the cellar. I used Bryn's code to open the secured entrance. I was being reckless by entering the room twice in one day. If my brother Jasper had nothing better to do than monitor all the family estates for movement, then it wouldn't be difficult to figure out that a family member had visited the mansion. Knowing my brother, he kept tabs on Bryn and Spencer. He could've easily figured out it was me and set Nestor or one of his other investigators on my trail to find me. Our investigators were the best in the business, so they would've found me. The only reason I could think of why they hadn't located me yet was because Jasper wasn't looking. That was why I figured it was safe to go to the mansion, get masks, and accept the invitation to Bartleby Leonard's masquerade party.

Bartleby threw the same masquerade party every year. He changed the cities, though. Last time I attended, it was in LA—the year before that, Manhattan. I'd introduced Si to Bartleby during a trip to St. Barths. As far as Bart was concerned, I'd dropped off the face of the Earth, so he'd invited Si, who accepted the invitation and handed the details over to me. Si didn't like Bart, which was why he'd never attended any of the guy's parties. Si referred to him as a pretentious, lazy narcissist.

Regardless, Bart knew how to throw a hell of a shindig. When Penina told me she'd been stuck in the hospital, unable to have any real fun since her residency started, I figured that night, I would score some forever points with her by showing her the time of her life.

That was negligent of me. The same people ran in that circle. Year after year, they traveled the globe, partying, getting high and drunk, fucking each other, and doing it repeatedly. Of course someone would recognize me.

I'd gone through a period in my life in which all I wanted was diversion. It usually occurred after I found my ex Gina and my brother Spencer fucking again, or after being seduced by Julia, the woman who was supposed to marry my oldest brother, Jasper. Her father and our father had insisted on the marriage. Jasper was frank about the fact that he would never love her or touch her. And she was scared as hell of him, like everybody else who didn't know him like we did. However, I had no idea how I kept getting pulled into Julia's evil web back then. She was poisonous and got off on sucking the blood out of me—and vice versa, I guessed.

That was then, though. As I stood in front of the glass cabinets filled with exotic masks, I accepted the fact that I had become a different man. The rigorous training I'd undergone to become a top neurosurgeon and the connections I'd made with my patients and colleagues had made me Jake Sparrow, the man I could see in the mirror and be proud of.

I put the golden wolverine mask back on the stand. It had belonged to my father.

"Fuck," I muttered as I closed the glass case and continued squeezing the knob. It had suddenly dawned on me that he'd probably used it during one of his salacious parties where pot-bellied, balding, and dick-shriveling old guys overdosing on Viagra were fucking underage girls. Shit, and I even let Penina wear one of them.

The idea of allowing his essence to encounter Penina made me sick. That was why I had to see her, watch her, wait until I knew for sure that the vexing ghost that haunted everything he'd touched hadn't disturbed her sleep.

I had Kirk take me back to the penthouse, and I dropped off my suit at the front desk. Since then, I'd been sitting in the dark, listening to her snores, guarding her body and soul, envying her tranquility, and waiting for her to once again squeeze the pillow a little tighter.

She'd cling to me the same way whenever I slept with her until I carefully loosened her grip. I only freed myself because her touch always made me want more of her. I could've kissed and made love to Penina every second of the day and all through the night. I also wanted to laugh with her, talk with her, eat with her, and even be in the OR with her. I imagined her with me during visits with my siblings. Penina was strong and smart and could hold her own, especially against Bryn and Spencer.

Spencer ...

Currently, he was in politics. Of all people, Spencer was looking to be a senator. I would've shaken my head if I hadn't had to sit still so that Penina wouldn't detect the shifting energy in the room. It was amazing what the human spirit and soul continued discerning when the body was unconscious. One superfluous move, and Penina could wake up and discover me watching her.

She snored again and flipped onto her right side, taking the pillow with her. I wondered why she needed to hold on so tightly to something. Shockingly, I didn't want to run away from her because of it. I wanted Penina to need me and desire me. If she knew who I truly was, whose blood was coursing through my veins, would she want me just the same?

Probably not.

I fought the urge to kiss her forehead. I'd done it before while she was sleeping. She didn't wake up. I rose slowly to my feet and took a step toward her. Penina stirred.

"Christmas brother," she muttered and hugged her pillow tighter.

I froze. My head turned light as my ears rang. *What the hell did she just say?*

Two Hours Later

. . .

On the treadmill, I pumped my arms and legs, trying to run worry out of my system. I couldn't take jumpiness and lack of focus with me into the OR that morning. I hadn't kissed Penina as I'd intended. Instead, I'd gone straight to the hospital. *Did she say what I thought I heard?*

I pushed the acceleration button and ran faster while trying to talk myself into a different conclusion. Christmas was about four months away. She could've said, "distant brother," or "distant mother," which made sense, since we'd had a conversation about her mother a few days ago.

I chose to take that conclusion and run with it. I had to. It was important that my mind competed with no thoughts beyond Leonard Moreau's brain. He was my first and only surgery of the day.

Damn, I wish I could sleep.

My eyes throbbed. Leonard's surgery was less than two hours away. I turned up the speed again and ran faster. My body was tired but strong. As for my mind, as soon as the scalpel was in my hand and I was in the thick of a procedure with my team in tow, it became sharp and aware. I could generally go five days straight without sleep. On the sixth day, I would crash for four to five hours then wake up choking and gasping, unable to remember what made me do it.

The treadmill beeped and slowed. When it came to a stop, I had run six miles and was soaked in sweat. My body wanted to drag, but my brain felt invigorated. It was time to shower, dress, and take that damn tumor out of Leonard's brain.

One and a Half Hours Later

My only surgery of the day was on the horizon, and I was tooled up and ready to go. I knew what approach to take to get the aggressive cancer. I had spent months studying the growth. According to the morning scans, Leonard Moreau had followed the regimen I'd given him to a tee. The prescribed daily lifestyle changes had kept the cancer from metastasizing. Since Leonard had done his job, it was time for me to do mine.

I walked down the corridor, chin up, looking people in the eye, and nodding sharply at those I passed. I answered their greetings with a strong "Good morning" as I ran Leonard's story through my mind. The forty-two-year-old male had become my patient the day after I arrived in New Orleans. Three previous doctors from separate medical institutions around the country had advised him that the tumor was operable but that there was a one hundred percent chance that removing it would make him blind. He would also lose all sensory function and some motor function. His growth had a mean-ass streak, expanding to other regions of his brain. He was lucky to still be walking and talking and able to search to save his own life. Leonard had two daughters. He wanted to live to be with them for as long as he could.

The patient had been on the verge of going bankrupt by the time he reached me, but he was fighting too hard to stay alive to be depressed about it. It just so happened that on his flight from Maryland back to New Orleans, Leonard suffered two seizures. Since he'd been tagged as a disabled passenger with high-priority special needs, he'd been put in first class. Some people called it luck, but I'd been a surgeon long enough to know that it was the will of God that Leonard had been seated next to Justin Jones, an oncologist and colleague of mine from Australia. As soon as their flight landed, Justin called me and told me Leonard's story, including the in-flight seizures, and Leonard came directly to the hospital so I could take a look at him.

"Don't worry about cost," I told him.

I owned the fucking hospital. When I'd bought it, the facility was new and going under fast due to mismanagement. Si had called and asked if I was interested in buying it. He had said the board wanted to save face, so the quieter they could keep the transaction, the better. I made myself think like my eldest brother Jasper would, considering the pros and cons. The next day, we started the purchasing process. The record showed that Pete Sykes was the new owner.

I'd reached the part of the surgery when I envisioned myself being the cancer, traveling through the brain, wrapping myself around tissue, nerves, and blood vessels. The more aggressive I was, the more harm I wanted to inflict. I dared any surgeon to try to stop me, puffing my chest, gritting my teeth. I was a fucking rabid wolf coming for Dr. Sparrow.

"What are you going to do, Jake?" I muttered.

The brain was mightier than brawn. I was going to outthink the cancer. For the past six days, I'd been practicing an extraction technique, using digital technology. I'd been successful at removing the cancer from a 3-D graphic of Leonard's brain sixteen times, after previously failing three hundred ninety-six times. I was more than ready to do it for real.

I stepped into the room, which housed the care station, and stopped in my tracks. There she was, standing with my team—Penina Ross. She was bright-eyed, beautiful, and seductive, and no way in hell was she going into that OR with me and the others.

I STARTED WALKING AGAIN, STRETCHING MY NECK from side to side, getting the prickling out of it. "Dr. Ross," I said, losing control of my pitch. "What are you doing here?"

Penina smiled pleasantly. "I'm on your team today, Dr. Sparrow." She sounded as if the previous night hadn't occurred and not a stitch of her heart was broken.

I set my eyes on Deb, who stood beside her. The way she looked at me, she was daring me to kick Penina off my team.

All eyes were on me. I'd worked in enough hospitals to know that everyone knew I'd purposely avoided Penina Ross, and they were too intelligent not to know why. I might as well have announced that I'd been fucking her and we'd been practically living together.

It dawned on me that I'd been doing it wrong. I had to keep her close, be nice, and treat her like I did the rest. So I kept a cool head as I said, "Then let's prepare to scrub in."

After a short pause, my team started to disperse, including Penina. I fought the urge to call her, escort her to my office, and just fuck her so I could get it out of my system. I loved the way her skin glowed in the morning, and I could smell her from across the room. Her natural scent would fill the OR, making it harder for me to concentrate on Leonard. *Fuck!* I was fucked.

I closed my eyes and filled my lungs with sterile hospital air, the best kind of air. *Penina Ross.* Fuck, my dick was hard.

"Dr. Sparrow, are you all right?" Deb asked.

I opened my eyes and narrowed them at her. She had a way of looking at me as if she wanted to scratch my eyes out.

"Do I bother you, Dr. Glasgow?" I asked.

Her indifferent shrug was like another slap in the

face. "You're the surgeon of our dreams, but I don't understand why you don't like my residents."

I avoided sniffing cynically. She meant one resident in particular.

Smiling warmly, I said, "I like your residents, Dr. Glasgow. You've done a fine job whipping them into shape."

She slammed the flimsy file folder on the countertop closed. "Dr. Ross is our best. And I don't understand how you don't want to team up with the best." A dare flashed in her eyes. "Unless you're just that insecure."

It was an insulting jab, but I'd come across Deb's type before. She was an overworked employee who was emotionally tied to those in her charge as if they were an extension of herself. She had taken my decision to keep my distance from Penina personally, and I liked it and respected it. And also, she liked me, which was fine. She would get over me in a matter of months.

"Dr. Glasgow, I agree with you regarding Dr. Ross. I promise, I've heard you. I'll do better." I nodded sharply and headed for the battle with my team versus a Godzilla of a cancerous tumor.

I had to pretend Penina wasn't in the OR, even though she'd been standing next to me for three hours, following my instructions precisely. I had to fool myself into thinking it wasn't her smell that I had to fight the urge to bathe in. At one point, I had to stand behind her to see what she was viewing. My dick accidentally brushed against her, and she tensed up.

"Relax, Dr. Ross," I said. "You're doing fine."

It appeared as if no one in the room could detect what was happening between us. In my entire career, I'd never been so fucking distracted during surgery. That was it—Penina could never be in the OR with me again. And she had to stop pushing the matter and have some fucking mercy on me.

"Good job, Dr. Ross," I said after she carefully removed the part of the tumor I'd directed her to extract. "Get settled at position three and watch for any possible surrounding nerve and tissue damage on the monitor."

I could relax a bit as she gave me some space. I had done my surgical-instructor duty for the day. I would've asked Penina to get the hell out of my OR, but I wanted her to stay near. I had changed my mind about what I'd said to her the previous night.

After the procedure, we needed to fuck first then talk about how to make our relationship work.

Knowing what I intended to do regarding Dr. Ross, I was able to ignore her enough to concentrate solely on beating the tumor in Leonard's brain.

CHAPTER TWENTY-TWO

PENINA ROSS

The surgery was nine hours and twenty-three minutes long. That was good timing. The procedure ended two hours ahead of expectations, and not only did the patient survive, but Jake was able to get all of the tumor. He made no mistakes and directed his team as if we were a fine-tuned machine.

He was so hot, and sexy as hell. Watching Jake work was such a turn-on. I could hardly believe we had broken up the previous night, because I wanted him so bad that my pussy twitched whenever I thought about him. He wanted me too. I was certain of it. I caught him looking at me from time to time, and all I saw in his eyes was pure lust. Maybe we could have a completely sexual relationship. I wouldn't need to know his real name or where he came from or where he planned to go once his cover was blown. Some of our nosiest colleagues would eventually figure out his real story.

"Penina, to my office, please," Jake said.

When I snapped my attention to the door of the call room, it was closing, and he was gone. I'd been freshening up after surgery, and I quickly ran deodorant under my other armpit, tossed the stick back into my locker, slammed it shut, and went to go see what Jake wanted.

As I walked down the hallway and crossed the bridge that led to the offices, I thought about where we would have all the sex to fulfill the sort of relationship I was going to propose to him. A hotel room would be neutral ground. He would pay for one night and I another. Even though he was obviously loaded, I would feel like a cheap call girl if he paid for all the nights.

I stopped in front of his office and balled my fist to knock but froze to think about how I should do it. I didn't want him to think I was eager to see him, even though I was. *And what's wrong with eager anyway, Pen?* I twisted my mouth thoughtfully. Still, I didn't want to come off that way. So I took a deep breath to cool my anxiety and gave the door three strong knocks.

"Come in," he said.

I paused, taking note of his tone. He was sharp and professional. Perhaps he wanted to speak to me about my performance in the OR that day. It had been stellar, as far as I was concerned. Whenever my gaze had connected with his, it sent my heart racing, but other than that, I was in rare form, and I was ready to defend my performance when I pushed the door open.

Jake stood at the window, looking out over the courtyard.

"Penina, have a seat on the sofa," he said without turning to acknowledge me.

Choked by trepidation, I crossed my arms and sat. "Is everything okay?"

I waited for him to say something. Finally, he cleared his throat.

"My need for you won't go away. If you don't mind, I'd like you to stay in the penthouse until we figure out what to do next," he said.

I smashed my lips together, increasing tension. Boy, did he sound entitled to get what he wanted when he wanted it. "To do next?" I asked, shaking my head. "Do you remember last night?"

"Of course, Penina," he said in a strained voice.

It was the perfect moment to share with him my idea of how we should proceed. But watching his towering presence and hearing his voice made me know for certain that I wouldn't be able to give him my body and soul through sensual sex and not fall in love with him. What was happening between Jake and me was different from any relationship I'd been in or contemplated. Something in me was drawn to him as if I had magnets in my heart, brain, and pussy that could only connect to Jake Sparrow.

"Then what do you want from me, Jake?" I sighed as I rose wearily to my feet, ready to leave at a moment's notice. I was exhausted. We'd had a long surgery, a long night, and frankly, I would've been okay continuing our discussion the next day.

He finally turned around. His pale eyes beaming at me were translucent yet so opaque. Then he moved toward me, and not only had I forgotten how tired I was, but I neglected to breathe. Jake stopped in front of me. His presence washed over me, and I felt as though I were floating in the atmosphere on a perfect, cloudless, and warm day.

What is this feeling?

Is it ...

It is ...

He was home.

Our eye contact remained strong. The wings of butterflies fluttered in my chest and stomach.

Jake's hands shot up but stopped short of coming down on my shoulders. Instead, he let his arms fall along his sides. "Penina, what you've suspected of me is clearly the case. I'm hiding a lot about myself. But I'm not ready to disclose what that is. I can't. My life would change if I did, and I like my life, but not if you're not in it."

I shook my head slightly. *Shit.* He'd just confessed he indeed had secrets, and more importantly, he didn't want to reveal them.

I scratched the back of my neck, coming up with a list of the sorts of secrets he might have that I could absolutely never accept. "Are you married?"

He chuckled. "No, Penina. I'm not married."

"Have you committed murder?"

He furrowed his brow.

I jerked my head back. "Is that a *yes*?"

"We're surgeons. You can't ask a surgeon that question. I have regrets. Earlier in my career, I could've done better and saved a life instead of losing that life."

"Yes," I said, nodding and sighing with relief. "That's a valid point."

He smirked. "Is it?" His eyebrows flicked up twice.

I touched my face to feel my smile. "Mm-hmm."

"Penina," he whispered and curved an arm around me.

"Yes." I sighed, my head soaring to somewhere beautiful again.

His eager lips found mine. Although the energy by which his lips seized mine was intense, his tongue worked sensually, delicately tasting its way deeper into my mouth.

Pausing for air, we gazed longingly into each other's eyes. His warm breath slid against my parted lips, and I breathed him into my lungs. Then, in a sensual collision, our tongues pushed, stroked, tasted, and laved. Jake's erection was so stiff it could be used as a hammer. He shoved his hand into my pants, and I shoved mine into his. I was right—hard, like steel.

Our hands feverishly sought to get past our clothes. He sank his fingers into my pussy while smashing my clit. I moaned in his mouth as I pumped his shaft like a piston.

Knock, knock, knock.

Shit.

We became very still with our dizzied gazes posted on each other.

Jake put a finger against his lips, signaling for me to remain silent. I didn't move a muscle. His eyebrow arched as he carefully but quickly lifted my arm, taking my hand out of his pants. I felt the absence of his hard dick against my palm and his slippery tip on my fingers. Jake tiptoed to the door and very slowly pushed the button to lock it. Whoever was on the other side knocked again.

"Dr. Sparrow?" Deb called.

I slapped a hand over my mouth, stifling a gasp. Jake remained silent. After a few more seconds, her rapid footsteps scurried away.

Jake and I exchanged looks that said we were happy to dodge that bullet. I pressed my lips together, forcing myself not to laugh. He waggled his eyebrows then walked over and wrapped me in his arms again. I succumbed to his hard body and the nearness of his beautiful face by drifting closer against him, interlacing my fingers through his hair.

His finger gently traced a line down the side of my face. "I want you in my life, Penina." Since we had almost been caught with our tongues in each other's mouths and our hands in the other's pants, he kept his voice low.

I nodded. "We'll talk?" I asked, watching my volume as well.

"Tonight, I'll tell you everything you need to know about me. It's not an easy choice I'm making, but I'm choosing to trust you, Penina. Can I trust you?"

It took a moment for me to register that he was asking a question. "No one's better at keeping secrets than I am."

Jake nodded gently. We stared into each other's eyes.

He wet his lips while focusing on his finger trailing down the side of my neck. "I want to fuck. What about you?" he asked.

I tipped my head back, sucking in air sharply between my teeth, allowing the divine tickling sensation on my neck to rouse my pussy. "You get right to the point, don't you?"

"We don't have much time. Deb's looking for either me or you."

I waggled my eyebrows. "Okay. Then let's fuck."

Without pause, Jake tugged my pants and my panties down until they bunched around my feet. As I stepped out of my garments, he pulled his down and freed his cock from his underwear. The cold office air on our newly exposed skin did nothing to quench our desire.

Our mouths luxuriated in feverish kissing as he hoisted me off the carpet with one arm. In one smooth move, I wrapped my thighs around his waist as he crammed his dick into my sensitive pussy with his other hand.

"Huh!" I gasped, keeping my voice as low as possible while his manhood plunged through my wetness. That felt good.

Jake sat me down on his desk. The hard wood was cold against my ass. I arched my back as our gazes explored each other's faces.

Then he closed his eyes, raking his front teeth across his bottom lip, and whispered, "Mmm. You feel so damn good. I'm going to come too fucking fast."

His thickness filled me up so that even as we waited in a moment of high anticipation, my sensitive sex was eager for him to get started.

I moaned. "Oh, Jake," I whispered, impatiently lifting my hips toward his cock. I couldn't take it. My lust was aflame.

That one action was the match that lit his fire. Jake reached between my ass and the hard desk, grabbing the rounds of my cheeks. Suddenly, he sipped air sharply between his clenched teeth as he indulgently shifted my pussy against his erection.

"Oh," he repeated in whispers as the euphoric look on his face exhibited just how much he wanted to blast off inside me.

My thighs trembled as I felt the tingling and throbbing with each stroke.

"I'm going to come," he whispered.

Caught in euphoria, I tilted my head back, breaths deep and soft, said, "Me too," and curved my hips more toward the action. Jake would hold on if he knew I was almost there.

"It's close." I sighed.

The sensation built and built.

"Come on, baby," he whispered, releasing a trembling sigh. Jake gave it to me at the right pace.

"It's … ha!" My orgasm burst into existence, then it spread like wildfire.

"Shit." Jake grunted and quivered, releasing himself after knowing I had done the same.

I RESTED THE SIDE OF MY FACE ON HIS SHIRT-COVERED chest, and his hands rubbed my back while we held each other, giving our bodies a moment to cool. One thing was for certain ... we were definitely on again. We looked at each other with silly postcoital grins. Then we engaged in more sensual head-spinning kissing before we cleaned ourselves with Kleenex and headed out for rounds.

I exited his office first, but I didn't take the direct path back to the care station. I knew Deb well. If she suspected Jake and I were alone in his office, then she would make sure she saw which hallway I used to enter the care station.

The medical complex was one of those modern monstrosities. The care station was set in the middle of the sixth floor, and four hallways poured into the area. One corridor led to attendings' offices. That meant Deb would be positioned in a spot where she could see me walking from that direction, all woozy from my quickie with our sexy new attending. I was pretty much on cloud nine and would be for the next hour, so I walked in the opposite direction of the care station and took the stairs down to the courtyard, where Lonzo, the guy who ran the coffee cart, gave me a free latte because I'd left my wallet in my locker. When I casually strolled into the care station, sipping my hot latte, it appeared as if I had taken a restorative break.

Once I saw where Deb was positioned, I

constrained a smirk. I had been right about her. I also pretended not to see her when she looked at me in surprise. That was the problem with carrying on a secret relationship in a hospital. Everyone who worked there was too smart. At some point, our colleagues would figure out that Jake and I were getting it on and, to my surprise, falling for each other on a deep level. However, that wasn't the time.

My shift ended, and I completed handoffs. I played Jake's game and pretended to not see him as I said goodbye to everyone in the vicinity.

"Dr. Ross," he said after I had turned my back on him.

The sound of his voice calling my name blasted through me like an electrical current.

I turned to face him. "Yes, Dr. Sparrow," I said.

His smile was pleasant and completely casual. "Thanks for the great assist today."

"You're welcome." My tone matched his.

I didn't observe anyone after that exchange, even though I could sense Angela and Deb watching us. *Who are we fooling anyway?* Our attraction for one another was like fluorescent red light streaking through the room. They knew something was going on between us. They could probably feel it.

I still had that floaty feeling as I walked through the busy lobby. Jake and I would do it again as soon as we were in the penthouse together. I was making plans to strip out of my clothes, take a bath, and wait in the tub until Jake got home, when I walked past Rich. He pretended not to notice me, which was sort of a bummer. I thought we at least liked each other enough to be cordial. I rolled my eyes as I ambled through the sliding glass doors. As usual, the outside air instantly reminded my body how exhausted I was.

Just as I finished a yawn, a tall and slender man with dark hair and brown eyes obstructed my path. I grimaced because I recognized him from somewhere. Then the tension released from my body as I recalled him pushing the button for the elevator the previous night.

"Dr. Ross?" he asked.

"You're Jake's driver," I said.

He held out a hand. "I'm Kirk."

"Nice to officially meet you, Kirk," I said as we shook.

"Jake would like for me to take you to the penthouse."

I wondered if he knew Jake's real identity. There was no way I was going to ask. I wouldn't dare put Kirk in the position of informing on his employer. Plus, Jake had said he would tell me the truth about himself that night.

So I forced a tired smile. "Lead the way?"

He smiled back, and I followed him to a black luxury sedan parked against a red spot along the curb in front of the hospital.

"No ticket for you?" I asked, grinning as he opened the door.

He sniffed. "Sometimes. But …" He hesitated. "They're all in Dr. Sparrow's name."

We both chuckled as I slid into the back seat. I could have sworn he was going to say something else or call Jake by another name.

As the vehicle pulled away from the curb, I saw Rich standing on the sidewalk, watching us like a hawk from afar.

I COULD'VE WALKED TO THE PENTHOUSE, BUT I WAS happy I hadn't. My head was heavy with exhaustion, and my throat felt scratchy. I usually kept my immune system robust by taking vitamins and drinking chamomile-and-echinacea tea with lemon and honey throughout the day, but I hadn't downed one cup since Jake came into my life. Resting my head on the seat, I thought that would be the first thing I did when I arrived at the penthouse—call room service and have them make me a cup of tea. I loved room service. One call and voilà. I could be spoiled by it.

My cell phone dinged in my bag. I had a text message, and believing it was Jake, I dug my device out. But the message was from Jamie, letting tenants know we could return to our apartments.

I pressed my lips together as I realized I was practically living with Jake. *What is he to me? My new boyfriend?* We would certainly have to define the parameters of our relationship later that evening when he came home.

"When he comes home," I whispered just to hear how the words sounded outside of my head.

Going to bed without him had been so painful the previous night. After the party, I took off my mask, jewelry, dress, and shoes, and put them back in the big box. I refused to cry as I washed the makeup off my face. While studying my reflection in the mirror, I noticed that I looked the same. Even though so much had changed in my life, I was still the same Penina, and I liked that.

Know thyself. Always try to be aware of who you are. It's not going to be easy, but do it.

Those words, spoken in my mother's voice, came back to me before I turned away from my reflection. I couldn't remember if she'd said them to me, but someone had.

Regardless, a yawn made me stop trying to figure out the mystery of the speaker, and I crawled into bed, thankful I hadn't canceled my shift for the day. Knowing myself was why I was able to look Jake in the eye that morning and dare him to pull me off his service. If he wanted out of our personal-slash-sexual relationship, that was fine, but our professional relationship was not up for debate. He was the best neurosurgeon in the hospital, and because of it, I was obligated to learn whatever the hell he could teach me. But I'd had no idea we'd end up back together before the day was over.

Kirk stopped the car in front of the elevator in the parking garage. He opened my door then pushed the button for the elevator. While he waited with me, we talked about how nice and warm the evening was. Not too humid, thankfully. He couldn't wait until the summer ended. I yawned. He told me to have a nice rest of the day, then I rode up to the penthouse floor. I closed my eyes, letting myself feel the smooth ascension. I would soon be back in Jake's domain and, after that afternoon, solidly back in his world. The elevator dinged. My eyelids fluttered open as the doors separated. Then I gasped as my heartbeat raced at the sight of a woman I'd never seen before.

FOR SEVERAL MOMENTS, WE SAID NOTHING AS WE studied each other. I sensed I had taken her by surprise as well. The woman was very attractive in the way that most women who put an effort into their appearance were. Eyeliner was applied thickly on her lower and upper eyelids. Her lipstick and blush were bloodred, but somehow the overpainting seem to complement her ivory skin. She wore an emerald cotton sundress without a bra. It was the sort that looked as if it cost a lot of money. Her short dark hair, cut into cute layers, went perfectly with her bare shoulders and swanlike neck.

She was the first to ask, "Who are you?"

"I'm Dr. Ross. Who are you?" I finally managed to say.

She snarled then crossed her arms. "Gina, and this is my apartment. What are you doing here, Dr. Ross?" She said it with such spite.

"Oh," I said, sighing in relief. "You're Jake's friend."

The woman chuckled. "Jake. That's right. I heard that's what he's calling himself these days."

I couldn't move a muscle. "I'm sorry?"

"Asher. He's calling himself Jake Sparrow, I heard. But he's Asher Nathaniel Christmas, and I'm his girlfriend. So again, who the hell are you?"

I thought she said her name was Gina, but I was so shocked that I barely heard her. I didn't want to know it, really. The world "girlfriend" kept repeating in my head, taking root in my heart. The moment I knew would come had arrived. Jake, or Asher, had disappointed me. And the worst—or maybe the best—part about it was that I was relieved that we could finally stop pretending that he wouldn't leave me. Everyone loved me and left me, including my own mother. Tears in my eyes, I apologized for infringing on her property and asked if I could pack my things before leaving.

She remained smug and cold when she said, "Make it quick."

What a bitch.

The tears fell freely as I secured my computer and mail from the other day. I shoved the clothes I'd worn on the night of the fire into my bag too. I hadn't realized how smoky they smelled. I needed to do laundry. The fact that I was thinking about that at such a humiliating, confusing, and heartbreaking moment made me feel worse.

After I was all packed up and on my way out, she stood by the elevator. I didn't want to see her again or that smirk on her face. I wasn't weak, but I knew when to and when not to fight. She had won. Jake or Asher had already let me know he'd bought the penthouse for a woman he was close to.

"Whatever Asher has with you, forget about it. He's not well," she said. "My advice is that you bow out now before he breaks your heart later. Once his brothers know where he is, they're coming to get him."

My frown deepened, not because she was being a stellar bitch who I wanted to punch in the mouth, or because she kept calling Jake 'Asher,' but because I faintly remembered Eloise mentioning a Christmas brother. Then I recalled the news show I'd been watching the other day. They were discussing a politician named Spencer Christmas. One of his critics had called him a billionaire from old money. I could hardly believe how all the parts were falling into place.

Caught in a trance, I stepped into the elevator.

"Down," Gina said, smashing the button. She scowled at me until the doors closed between us.

As I walked through the lobby, the people I was used to greeting said their hellos, and I put on my happiest face, not giving any indication that we were saying our final goodbyes. Then I was out on the sidewalk, walking back to my place, feeling as if my hot and fast relationship with Jake, or Asher, had come full circle.

Before I reached my building, I received another text, once again thinking it was the man I considered my ex-lover. I looked at my phone, curious to hear if his self-proclaimed girlfriend had told him what happened at the penthouse. But it wasn't Asher. It was my aunt.

Found your mother. Come.

CHAPTER TWENTY-THREE

PENINA ROSS

I booked a seat on a flight to Tampa that was taking off in two and a half hours and then called a cab. The driver was to arrive in half an hour. I packed fast, trying not to forget what I needed for a two-day stay in Tampa, Florida, while attempting to see clearly through my teary eyes. My suitcase was almost packed when I remembered that I had to call Deb. I didn't want her to sense that I'd been crying, so I pulled myself together as much as I could before getting her on the phone. I told her I needed two days off.

"What's going on? Are you okay?" She sounded highly concerned.

I closed my eyes to get a handle on my grief. "I

have to fly to Tampa, Florida, and identify my mom's body."

She gasped and apologized profusely for my circumstances. Although she had nothing to do with my mom's death, I accepted her apology and asked if she wouldn't mind keeping my situation between the two of us.

"Of course. Your privacy will be respected."

I thanked her. Deb wished me safe travels, and we ended our call.

Part of me wanted to call and report to Jake what had happened in his penthouse. That would've been the mature thing to do. Jake had been ready to tell me everything about himself, which more than likely would've included the information Gina had hurled in my face. I was blessed with a sharp intuition, and I recognized a spiteful person when I encountered one, so I wasn't convinced she was Jake's girlfriend. Her eyes had been shifting when she said it, and that indicated deception. Also, the energy in her body meant she was desperate to claim him. I was a threat to her. I probably should've stayed and held my ground.

With at least ten minutes to spare before the cab was to arrive, I had all that I needed in my suitcase, and I decided to wait for the driver out front. It was a warm and lively late afternoon. Cars raced up and down the road, and people shuffled along the sidewalks on both sides of the street.

But none of the activity distracted me from my thoughts about Jake. Maybe he had left Gina without ever officially breaking up with her. Anyone who was running from the law and would go through the effort of changing their identity was not only fickle, but also content with being the type of person no one could rely on. Jake and I had chemistry, that was for sure, but the more I learned that he was not the sort of person I could trust, the more I felt our connection fading.

I'd concluded that Gina was one jilted girlfriend too many when my suitcase and I plopped into the back seat of the taxi. It was time to focus on the new subject of my heartache—my mother. Aunt Christine wanted to meet me at the airport, but since I would be arriving in Tampa after ten p.m., I told her I would catch a cab and meet her at the hotel where she'd booked a room for the both of us.

"A real cab and not one of those services where you're putting your safety into the hands of an unvetted average Joe?" she asked.

Even though my tears were still rolling, I smiled a little. "Yes, a real taxicab."

The thought of not being alone made me happy, and I was excited about seeing her. My aunt was odd, but she was family. In her own way, she loved me very much.

THE HUSTLE AND BUSTLE OF THE AIRPORT WAS AS miserable as I remembered it. I'd had no idea so many people wanted to fly to Florida at eight thirty at night. I had never been a happy traveler. It was the getting there that made me irritable.

I was still scowling once I made it to my window seat. By the time the last person boarded, I realized how lucky I'd been. The seat between me and the nice lady who smelled like gardenias and was knitting remained empty. The extra space in the middle and the fact that I was seated beside the perfect traveling companion relaxed me.

I pressed my head against the window, remembering a story Aunt Christine had told me once about my first Christmas. She said she was so happy that I was in the world, and she bought me everything under the sun. Oddly, that was the end of the story. She never said what happened next—*at least I didn't think so*—and since I was only eight months old at the time, I couldn't remember the toys or whatever happened to them. But it was memories like that that made Christine weird. I always felt there was a lot about Mom and our past she wasn't sharing with me. However, I never pressed her for answers because deep down, I didn't want to lose hope that one day Mary Louise Ross would rise to the occasion and become better than some of the greatest moms in TV history. Of course, I knew those women didn't exist in real life, which meant my mother was more of the real thing than they were, but still, I kept hoping.

At some point during the flight, I fell asleep so hard that when the flight attendant shook me awake, the plane was nearly empty.

"Holy shit," I said, springing to life, spurred by a sudden hit of adrenaline.

It hadn't taken long after two days of getting too much rest to become completely exhausted again. Becoming a happy and successful surgeon required a work-life balance, and though I hadn't achieved it yet, I was determined to one day find the key and unlock the answer.

I grabbed my purse out of the bin and disembarked the aircraft as fast as I could.

My neck was stiff, my head throbbed, and my body was jerky as I walked to baggage claim and grabbed my luggage. Instead of a cab, I caught a shuttle to the hotel. It was even warmer and more humid in Tampa than it was in New Orleans.

All the thoughts about Jake were back with a vengeance. I pinched my lower lip, remembering his delicious mouth on mine. I could somehow smell his skin, hear his voice, and picture his infrequent smile. I'd turned off my cell phone for the flight and chose to keep it off afterward, knowing he would be calling me by then. I couldn't deal with trying to figure out whether he could be trusted. My eyelids grew heavier by the moment, and I couldn't stop yawning. I had to force myself to put Jake in a box and deal with him when I was emotionally able to. The next morning, Christine and I would drive over to the coroner's office together. Our appointment to identify the body of Mary Louise Ross was at ten a.m.

I tried to remember what my mom looked like. It was almost as if over the years, she'd become a faceless and bodyless aberration. My mom had been hooked on drugs, but which ones, I didn't know. A daughter should've known, but not me. I never knew much about her—where she grew up, how she met my father, nothing. I'd been sent to boarding school at the age of thirteen. My aunt Christine had paid for it. But before then, my mom used to drag me around the smallest and poorest towns in Southern California. I never knew why we moved so much. She never worked a real job.

Suddenly, my mind fed me snapshots of Mary and certain men. I remembered one guy her age who stared at me as if he wanted to cart me off and never bring me back. Mary had slapped him, pulled a gun on him, and told him to leave and never come back. Once he was gone, she gathered me into her arms. Later, we took a long bus ride to somewhere else, and she hugged me close as I slept on the way to our next destination. Or maybe she didn't hug me so close. I couldn't remember.

My sinuses tightened, and I squeezed the bridge of my nose as tears slid down my cheeks. Then I swiped my face, though I was the only passenger on the shuttle, so I didn't have to worry about sparking a fellow rider's curiosity.

I wondered why, after so many years, I had remembered that. Then another memory I always tried not to think about came to me. My mom used to always make me sit here or there, usually somewhere in public, while she ran an errand that took her away for hours. How a child could sit in one place for that long, I had no idea, but that was exactly what I had done. Her instructions were to never talk to or go anywhere with anyone unless that person was Aunt Christine. I must've asked her about a police officer, because she advised me to run away from them too. If she didn't return at the time she showed me on my watch, then I was to go into a store she had identified for me and tell the nice lady behind the cash register that I needed help and then give her an envelope.

She always made me keep that envelope folded and in my pocket, and I still had it. I had no idea why I'd kept it for so many years, but it was in my closet, inside a banker's box where my birth certificate, social security card, old report cards, and stuff like that were stored. I had never opened the letter. Just thinking about it made my scalp prickle. I took a deep breath in through my nostrils and let the air clear my brain. Maybe I was ready to read it. As I released the breath, I decided to open the soiled and ragged envelope and read the contents as soon as I returned to New Orleans—or maybe not.

When the shuttle was driving among rows of hotels and busy multiple-lane streets, I knew the hotel was not far away, so I turned on my cell phone to call Christine. My device dinged and vibrated, letting me know I had several messages from Jake, but I purposely avoided looking for or listening to them. As soon as I saw that he had reached out to me several times, my heart and soul wanted me to forgive him. *Forgive him for what, exactly?* I didn't know. Perhaps I wanted contention in our relationship.

The appearance of Gina had complicated things in ways I never saw coming. My mind kept trying to convince me that he wanted to pick her over me. *See how she was dressed. See how put together she was from head to toe.* I wore comfortable doctor clothes on a daily basis. I'd shrunk in her presence earlier that day. I didn't think I owned a dress that could compete with the one she had on. Asher Christmas was a billionaire, and those kinds of guys lived in a different universe from mine.

Christine met me in the wide-open and well-lit lobby. The décor was gaudy with a lot of glass trying to pass for crystal chandeliers. As usual, when I first saw my aunt, I marveled at how stunning she was. Her skin was like fine porcelain, and her eyes were dark and mysterious. She had wavy brunette hair, and she was about two inches taller than I was. Basically, my aunt had the DNA of a 1980s supermodel. My mom had also been taller than I was. I wasn't short, standing at five feet eight, but I must have gotten my height from the man who gave my mother the sperm that made me. With looks like hers, one would think my aunt would flaunt them, but she never did. It was as if Aunt Christine didn't notice or care that she was a goddess.

When she saw me, she waved, then crossed and uncrossed her arms. "How are you?" she asked when I reached her.

I didn't know whether to initiate a hug or not. "I'm fine, and you?" As soon as the question left my mouth, I noticed her puffy red eyes and splotchy skin. Her day-old mascara was smudged as well. I'd seen too many faces that looked like hers not to know she'd been crying. So I initiated a hug, and she instantly wrapped her arms around me, holding me tighter than I had held her.

"You're shaking." Her voice broke. "You must be tired."

I nodded. "I am exhausted."

"Come on, let's get you to bed."

We walked side by side to the elevator. I was probably better at small talk than she was, but whenever I spent time with her, I always struggled with it. I had some questions, but most of them had to do with what the coroner's office had said. I also wasn't clear about whether she'd seen my mother's body. I wanted to know if there were signs of trauma. Even though the last time I'd seen my mom was at my high school graduation, I couldn't bear it if she had suffered a painful death.

"How are you feeling about all of this?" Christine asked as the metal doors of the elevator slid open.

I leaned against the handrail once we were securely inside. Then I frowned, mainly because of the waft of cheap cologne someone had left behind. "Do you know how she died?"

She sighed and cast her gaze on the scuffed-up floor. "No, I do not. They'll tell us everything after we identify the body."

I raised my eyebrows. "Then you haven't seen her yet?"

She shook her head then whimpered in a way someone did to keep themselves from crying. "But they explained how she looked. She was also wearing our mother's locket. She never took it off." By the last sentence, her voice had cracked.

Truthfully, I didn't know how to respond. I always thought that Christine was more pragmatic and stonier than how she was acting. I'd pictured her consoling me, not the other way around. Suddenly, the reason why my aunt would make sure she had my new address and phone number every time I moved made sense. Also, a handful of times a year, she would email me an article about new developments in neurology or something. I'd gotten a sense that relationships were hard for her and that was why she was an exotically beautiful, ultra-smart, and kind, but single woman. My aunt, like my mother, had some damage. However, regardless of her inner issues, she maintained a relationship with her niece because she loved her sister. The fact that my mom and her sister could've had a real relationship never occurred to me until then.

When I was thirteen years old, my aunt had saved my life and ensured a solid future for me when she put me in boarding school. Before then, even though my mom would go missing for days at a time, my attendance was pretty good. School had been my best babysitter. I had learned to wake myself up in the morning, get dressed, and walk to the bus stop. I didn't have to worry about food either. Every school I attended in California had free breakfast and lunch programs, and since my mom was never employed, I always qualified.

However, whenever the office started asking deeper questions about my home life, Mary would pull me out of that school and put me in another one, using fake addresses to enroll me in brand new districts. From the ages of seven to thirteen, I had attended so many schools that it made me sick in the stomach to count them. I would always remember the day Aunt Christine visited and saw that I was sleeping on a dirty mattress in the corner of a studio apartment and rotating three sets of clothes as my entire wardrobe. She and my mom never argued in front of me. They went out for a chat. That was what Christine called it—a chat. When they came back, I packed my things and went to a hotel with my aunt.

I would never forget how I felt, sitting in the front seat of her rental car. I was exhausted, mentally and physically. When I slept in a real bed that night, it was as if the cavalry had arrived.

The next morning, on our way to the mall to shop for clothes, I asked Christine if my mother would be joining us that day. I was used to Christine taking me out to spend time alone whenever she came to town.

"Sweetheart, you're flying back to the East Coast with me. You're going to attend the best boarding school in the world. They're excited to have you, and I know the principal, a lot of the teachers, and the guidance counselors personally." Her voice cracked when she said, "They're going to take of you, babe. I promise." Then she cleared her throat.

That was the first time I truly perceived how sad my mom had made my aunt by choosing to raise me the way she had. I imagined they had fought the night they went out to talk. And Christine was right —Heart of Grace Academy wasn't one of those miserable boarding schools with abusive nuns, teachers, and classmates. I went to school in a nurturing environment where the administration was quite aware of the way we girls, living away from our parents, would suffer. I owed my aunt everything.

So, seeing how devastated she was about my mom's death, I consoled her by rubbing her arm. "One step at a time, right?"

She watched me with watery eyes, smiling tightly. We would've hugged again, but the doors slid open.

CHAPTER TWENTY-FOUR

PENINA ROSS

We were staying in a two-bedroom suite. Each room was on either side of a step-down living room space and a small dining area with a table, a microwave, a Keurig coffee setup, and a case with snacks that could be charged to the room if either of us decided to treat ourselves.

Christine gave me time alone to unpack and shower the stickiness off my skin from the long day. As the water soaked my hair and poured down my face, it took my tears and the last scents of Jake I had left on me down the drain with it. I didn't know whether to be brokenhearted about Jake or my mother. Also, never had I felt as though family was something I could rely on until observing my aunt's grief.

Then there was my mom. I looked at the wall, wanting to punch it. I wasn't angry with my mom, though. I was infuriated with myself for not trying to find her. She might not have been perfect, but I was a doctor who was very capable of meeting my mom where she was. I was so willing to give her the grace and space to be human. The fact that she'd died without me being able to offer the unconditional love she deserved was on me.

I understood why people slapped themselves in grief or banged their heads against the wall. It was my fault, all my fault. I broke down and wept, shrinking against the corner of the shower, letting the water spray me in the face.

Finally, at some point, I picked myself up off the floor, feeling drained by the pain, and moved on with my night.

I blow-dried my hair then tied my tresses in a bun for sleeping. When I went into the comfortably lit living room to say good night to Christine, she was sitting on the sofa, marking what appeared to be a manuscript.

"Good night, Christine." My tone was apprehensive.

She looked up at me with a gentle smile. "You've been crying."

If I had spoken, I would've cried some more, so I nodded stiffly.

She patted the sofa beside her. "Could you sit for a while?"

I was so happy she had offered that I didn't hesitate before walking in front of the large piece of furniture and sitting. I let my shoulders slump and my chest cave in.

Smiling, Christine sat her manuscript on the coffee table. "You have a hefty job there, surgeon."

"Yes, I do."

"I heard you're the top resident at your hospital," she said.

My mouth fell open. "You checked on me?"

"All the time. You're my niece. I love you." Her smile caressed me again. "You used to be so exhausted during our visits while you were in college. Half the time, I didn't think you knew whether you were coming or going."

I smiled as I gazed down at my lap, sniffing and chuckling. "Those were hellish days."

"Yeah, well ... You're in a very important profession. Not everyone is built to cut open a skull and tinker with a brain."

She was still beaming at me, which was a refreshing reversal from earlier. I was the one who was bent out of shape.

"Sorry about earlier," she said with a sigh. "Seeing you again brought back so many memories. I'm just so happy you're here."

"Me too." I flicked my wrist. "And no apology necessary."

Christine nodded thoughtfully then hiked her legs up on the sofa cushion and crossed them, making herself comfortable. "You never asked about your mother. Why?"

My eyes grew wide as I sat up straight, taking a few moments to come up with the right answer. "I don't know. But ..." I sighed. "I didn't know much about her, that's for sure. Like, where did you both grow up?"

Suddenly, Christine threw her hands up, palms facing me. "Then we're really doing this?"

I jerked my head back slightly. "Doing what, per se?"

"You're finally inquiring about your mother. Because I made a vow to myself to never tell you anything until you asked."

Something within me shot up like a glowing stop sign. It also shouted, "Do not proceed," "Turn back," and "Enter at your own risk."

"Um …" I leaned toward her, frowning. "Do I want to know?"

She narrowed her eyes, studying me intently. "Do you?"

I felt as if she were giving me an out.

"I won't judge you if you'd prefer not to know," she said.

Then I closed my eyes and nodded, although I was sure I would rather have shaken my head.

AUNT CHRISTINE STARTED WITH WHERE THEY'D BEEN born. I hadn't known they were originally from Toledo, Ohio. Our grandparents, who were both dead, had been extremely religious.

"They swore—and they never swore, but they did swear that your mother and I were going straight to hell. Our sin was breathing, and they felt we had to spend every waking hour of the day repenting for being alive since we were conceived in sin and shaped in iniquity. I mean …" She sniffed and rolled her eyes. "That was a lot of sin."

I chuckled.

She smiled warmly. "I only told you that because

I want you to understand the rejection and emotional abandonment your mother and I faced. The fight for our sanity and individuality began on day one."

I hoisted my legs onto the couch and hugged them, resting my chin on my knees. "Mom never asked me to be anything but myself. Nor did she make me shoulder her pain. It was as if we were living in two different spheres, even though we were in the same room."

"May I speak frankly?" she asked.

"Sure."

She sat up straighter. "Your mother didn't want to fuck you up, even though she was fucked up. She …" Christine clamped her lips together, closed her eyes, and breathed in deeply through her nose. After a moment, she opened her eyes again. "At the age of twelve, your mother ran away from home. She was starved for love, like many children in her … our … position. And that was why she fell into the wrong hands."

"I never knew that," I said past the tightness in my throat.

"I'm six years older than your mother. She ran away a month after I went off to college. Our parents never looked for her. They believed that like the prodigal son, their twelve-year-old daughter would come back beaten and ravished by the world and ready to conform." She set her unfocused gaze on the window, seeing off into the night. "It took me years to forgive them. I first had to understand them so that I could acquire empathy toward them."

I was captivated as she went on to tell me how whenever she wasn't in class or studying, she tried to find my mother. For many years, it was as if my mom had fallen off the face of the Earth. They'd never had the same friends, but during summer vacations and spring and winter breaks, she would return to her hometown without visiting her parents and question all my mother's friends, asking if they'd heard from her or knew where she might be. No one knew anything. Then during her sophomore year in college, Christine was in her dorm room, studying for finals, when a knock came at the door.

"I'll never forget who it was." Her eyes filled with happy tears. "Penny Carter was her name, and she said to me that I had a guest. Mary wouldn't tell Penny her name, but Penny said that the girl was young, pregnant, and looked like me. I knew exactly who it was."

I pressed my hand over my heart. "She was pregnant with me?"

As Christine nodded, I did the math in my head. "Then she was only …"

"Fourteen," Christine said.

My jaw dropped, then I buried my head in my arms as tears streamed out of my eyes. "I didn't know," I whispered past my thick throat.

My aunt remained quiet while I cried. I recognized the silence that lingered in the air. It was the patient sort of space that those in the medical field allowed for expressing grief. After all, Christine was a psychologist.

I pulled it together the best I could while she went to retrieve a box of tissues. When she returned, I blew my nose and wiped my eyes.

"Better?" she asked.

I cleared my throat and nodded.

She leaned forward to make full eye contact with me. "Tears are restorative, so cry without restraint."

I chuckled as I smiled, and so did she.

"Would you like for me to continue?" she asked.

I took a cleansing breath then pulled my shoulders back. "Yes." I felt stronger and closer to my mother and aunt than ever.

"Okay." She sighed. "Well … Mary Louise looked older than a fourteen-year-old girl because what she had endured aged her considerably."

"Do you know what happened to her?" I asked.

Christine watched me with a long, pained look then broke eye contact. "She never wanted to talk about it. But whatever happened to her gave her terrible nightmares. And she never felt as though she was worth anything. You were her greatest accomplishment and a constant reminder of her shame." She pressed her lips together as her chin trembled.

That was very difficult for my aunt to say, and I put my hands in front of me as if in prayer. "Thank you for telling me the truth. I'm not hurt. I always knew I was a reminder of whatever occurred between her and my father. The way she looked at me—sometimes she would love me as if I were the only thing that mattered to her in the world, then sometimes she would watch me with revulsion."

Suddenly, Christine held out her hands for me to take. I hesitated as something hard arose in my heart. The emotion took me by surprise.

"Come on," she urged me.

I furrowed my brow. *Does she know what I was feeling?* Carefully, I placed my palms on hers.

"Sweetheart, I love you more than words could convey," she choked out. "As a doctor, you've learned a lot about the complexities of human nature, haven't you?"

I nodded softly as she gripped my hands firmer. "I've already decided to give my mother the grace and the space to be human," I said.

Aunt Christine held steady eye contact as she smiled. "Then that's all I can ask."

She stood and held her arms out. "Now let's hug."

I rose, and we gave each other a long, loving, and healing hug.

CHAPTER TWENTY-FIVE

JAKE SPARROW/ASHER CHRISTMAS

My adrenaline was through the fucking roof. I slammed my palm against the wall. "What did you say to her?"

Gina had to comprehend the cruelty of what she had done. I was falling in love with Penina fast and hard. And one interaction with Gina, and my relationship with Penina was back in the shitter.

Gina shook her head as if she was stunned. "Why do you care?"

My muscles quivered. "Why do I *care*?" I bellowed.

When Gina jumped, I knew I'd gotten through to her. "I told her this was my house. Because it is!" she shouted.

"She knew that already. What else did you say?"

She closed her eyes as she looked away from me. "That I was your girlfriend. I'm sorry, Ash. I just … I don't like her."

I shook my head. "What else?"

Gina frowned as though she didn't know what else to reveal.

"Did you tell her my real name?"

Her mouth tightened as she crossed her arms. That was my answer.

We had nothing else to say to each other after that.

I turned my back on her and smashed the elevator's down button. "When I get back, I want you gone."

"You bought this penthouse for me, remember?" she yelled at my back. "Don't you want to know why I'm here?"

"Not really."

"I'm sorry, Ash," she whined.

I got into the elevator and pushed the closed button. My anger expanded as I watched the doors slide together, taking care of getting her out of my sight. Plus, she didn't sound sorry. I hadn't seen Gina in six years. How she'd chosen to blow up my relationship with Penina was one of several reasons why I'd put distance between us. She was bad for my life.

I'd heard she was a swim coach for young girls and had been successful at it, and I'd thought her new legitimate status in society would've changed her, but what she had done to Penina, she had done for sport.

People would see me getting out of a hired car in front of Penina's building and knocking on her door at night, but I didn't care. I had planned on officially asking her to be my girlfriend anyway. I wanted to take her out and show off our new relationship at Nurse Peters's Midsummer's Eve party the next night. She would be my date.

I told Kirk to stay parked in front of the building. I'd tried to call Penina several times on the way over but was sent straight to voicemail. I'd never taken her for the avoidant type. When I tried to freeze her out of my surgeries, she remained persistent. I liked that about her. I thought for certain she would be fair enough to hear my side. That was why I was surprised she wasn't answering.

A handful of people were waiting for the elevator. I couldn't stand still while being flanked by a group of strangers, so I opted to run up the stairs, taking them two, sometimes three steps at a time. I knew what condo she lived in because when I learned we worked in the same specialty, I looked her up in the system.

I pushed the door open to the third-floor hallway and stamped down it, observing the apartment numbers until I found hers.

"Penina?" I kept knocking and calling to let her know it was me.

A door opened nearby. "Dr. Sparrow?" a female asked in a highly curious voice.

I glanced behind me then did a double take. "Dr. Agate?"

She shook her head. "Just Zara. I'm not a surgeon anymore."

I furrowed my brow. I knew Zara Agate's father, Dr. Arush Agate. He was a brilliant cardiothoracic surgeon. I had been looking forward to working with her, especially if she was even half as brilliant as her father. "Oh, sorry to hear it."

She folded her arms and shrugged. "Don't be."

"Zara," I said, garnering firm eye contact.

She leaned away from me then slightly turned her head to eye me cautiously. "Yes, Dr. Sparrow?"

"Where's Penina?" When I'd seen them together a while ago, I could tell they were close. She would definitely cover for Penina, but I was ready to convince her to tell me where Penina was, come hell or high water.

"I don't know." She raised her eyebrows. "Why are you looking for her?"

It was then and there that I knew she was telling me the truth. "I can't find her, and I need to find her."

"But why?"

"Because we work together."

"I know that."

"Do you know if she's home or not?" I snapped.

After taking a moment to study me, she sighed. "Well …" She checked her watch. "Pen is usually asleep by now. Sometimes she puts these earplugs in, or maybe she puts a mask over her eyes. Regardless, just give me a sec. We have keys to each other's flats."

I sighed with relief. "Thanks."

Zara shot me a fake smile. "You're welcome. But you know, you could've just said the two of you are seeing each other. Pen would tell me anyway."

I kept a straight face as she waited for my reaction.

She rolled her eyes. "Whatever. I'll be right back."

Once she was out of sight, I released the tension in my chest.

I STOOD IN PENINA'S BEDROOM, AND IT APPEARED AS IF wherever she'd gone, she had left in a hurry. Clothes were strewn across her bed. The bag she carried on a daily basis was also on the bed, and her laptop was still sitting on her desk.

"So, now that I've let you in, are you going to confirm that the two of you are involved?" Zara asked.

I'd almost forgotten she was standing behind me. "Yes," I said without hesitation.

"All righty then," she said, sounding shocked I'd been frank. "I knew it would happen, but not so soon. Pen's slow to get it, you know ..."

I wanted to know what she meant by Pen being slow to get it, but I felt pressured by needing to locate my missing girlfriend.

"Could you call her?" My tone was curter than I'd wanted to make it.

Zara tilted her head. "Oh, then she's avoiding you."

"Could you please call her?" I took the sting out of my voice that time.

She sighed briskly. "Sure," she said and used the cell phone she'd been holding the whole time to place the call. She put the device next to her ear, and after about ten seconds turned her back on me. "Pen, it's me, Z. Call me." Zara faced me again when she ended the call.

"You got her voicemail?" I asked.

"I'm certain she knows you're looking for her, Jake. Whatever you've done, she's pissed about it. When Pen gets angry or sad, she drops off the face of the Earth, if she's not on shift. I'd just give her some space, if I were you."

Frowning, I rapped my fingers against my thigh, contemplating what to do next.

Zara waved a hand before my face, perhaps thinking I was dazed, and said, "Dr. Sparrow, she'll call you when she's ready. Unless whatever you did was pretty hurtful. Was it?" She set her jaw.

I shook my head, though I wasn't saying no. What Gina had said to Penina hurt her deeply. But I wanted more time alone in Penina's apartment to search for clues as to where she might've gone. My gaze roamed around the space. I was sure in all the mess there was something that would point to where I could find Penina.

"Do you mind leaving me alone?" I asked.

Zara threw her hands up. "Yes, I do mind leaving you alone in Pen's apartment without her permission."

Fuck, she's going to be difficult. I had to settle

myself and think fast. First, I nodded empathetically. "Zara, I understand you're being a good friend. Yes, I hurt her. But when she hears from me, I'll be able to explain what happened, she'll forgive me, and you'll be invited to the wedding." I grinned.

Her neck jutted forward. "Wedding?"

I snorted. "That was a joke."

She grunted and twisted her mouth thoughtfully. I couldn't tell what she might be thinking.

"How badly did you hurt her?" she asked.

"Very bad."

"Who did you fuck?"

I jerked my head back, amazed she'd ask me that. "No one. Her. Only her."

Her mouth formed an *O*, then she slapped her hand over it. After a moment, she dropped her hand, cleared her throat, and said, "Knock on my door when you're done so I can lock up."

My temple ached from frowning. I wanted to know why she'd reacted that way. "Thank you," I said instead. Maybe I didn't want to know.

I watched her until she closed the door behind her. Then I went on a hunt, tracking Penina's steps. She had used the bathroom. Her face towel was still damp but drying. She'd probably left two hours ago.

Penina's computer had been shut down, so I powered it up.

"Fuck," I muttered after the machine finished booting. I needed a password to enter.

I looked in the wastebasket near her desk. It had a few crumpled papers. Then I saw her mail and checked the back of each piece.

"Bingo," I said after seeing the numbers FR1539. That was a flight number.

I pulled my cell phone out of my pocket and called up the flight number. Sure enough, Freedom Airline flight 1539 had left the airport at eight-thirty, heading to Tampa, Florida.

"What the fuck is in Tampa?" I whispered.

Deb would know.

DEB DIDN'T ANSWER HER PHONE. NEXT, I CALLED THE care station, and whoever answered the phone said that Deb was somewhere in the hospital but busy.

On the way out of Penina's apartment, I knocked on Zara's door, said, "I'm gone," and raced down the hallway.

Kirk drove me over to the hospital. I got out of the car and jogged across the quad, through the lobby, and down the hallway. I looked disheveled, which was why a couple of people asked if I was okay, but I didn't answer. No, I wasn't fucking okay.

When I made it to the care station, Dr. Baker was charting. She only looked up when I dropped my hand on the counter in front of her.

"May I help you, Dr. Sparrow?" she asked without looking at me.

I took a few deep breaths to make them even. "Do you know why Dr. Ross might be in Tampa, Florida?" I still sounded winded.

Finally, Dr. Baker lifted her head and leaned back. Her lips were slightly parted, as if she were lost for words. "Um, no, I don't know why she would be in Florida."

"Family? Friends?" I pressed.

She shook her head. "Her aunt lives in Massachusetts."

"Aunt? Do you have her number?"

"Um …" She narrowed her eyes. "I don't think … I mean …" Then she pointed. "There's Deb. Deb!"

"Dr. Baker," Deb said from behind me.

"Dr. Sparrow's looking for Penina."

"Sorry, can't tell you," Deb said, passing through the area like a streak of lightning.

I ran to catch up to her.

"Dr. Sparrow, why do you need Dr. Ross? If it's a resident you want, then …"

"No," I said and trotted ahead of her.

I walked backward, and she continued to walk forward until she stopped in her tracks.

"I want Penina."

"Penina?" Her tone indicated that she had detected the personal way in which I'd said Penina's name.

"Yes. Please tell me where she is."

Deb straightened her posture. "You know, you are very self-important, Dr. Sparrow. You act like you own the place."

I scratched my ear, fighting the urge to tell her that I did own the place, which meant that she had better start singing about where I could find the woman that I fucking loved or else. However, Deb was not the sort of employee a smart business owner pissed off. Without her, the internship and residency program would've crumbled a long time ago.

So I took a step back and steepled my fingers in front of my mouth. "I'm sorry you feel that way, Deb."

She tilted her head, studying me. "Are you?" She obviously wanted to fight. Perhaps she had some pent-up frustration with me.

"Yes. I am."

"She is in Tampa. Why?" I asked.

"You know she's in Tampa?"

"Zara told me."

Her lips twitched as if she'd stopped herself from saying something. "What's going on between the two of you?"

I swallowed. I had a split second to make a decision. Revealing our relationship to Deb was different from telling Zara. One was her friend, and the other was her boss. Penina would've liked to choose how she was going to break the news of our relationship to Deb. I wanted to sniff at that, though, since at the moment, I wasn't sure we were still in a relationship.

"Nothing," I said. *Fuck.* I wanted to tell her the truth. "Personal. Nothing personal. We share a patient, and I think she'd want to hear an update."

"What patient?"

"Leonard Moreau," I answered just as fast as she asked.

"Well …" Deb heaved a sigh. "She'll be back on Saturday, maybe." She shook her head. "I'm sorry, Dr. Sparrow, but I made her a promise."

I nodded. At least I knew Penina was not hurt. "Then an emergency came up?"

"Yes, sir," she said.

I took in a deep breath, bowed graciously, and said, "Thank you."

Deb narrowed her eyes suspiciously. "You're welcome," she said then tore down the hallway to do whatever she had set out to do before I got in her way.

I would have to wait until Penina's flight landed in New Orleans. I scratched my head, thinking of my next move. She must've booked a round-trip flight. Deb had said she was returning to work on Saturday, which meant she was flying in sometime tomorrow on Freedom Airlines. I only had two morning surgeries for the next day. I would send Kirk to the airport just in case her flight arrived while I was in the OR. When I was out, and possibly while she was in the air, I would have him pick me up and take me to the airport, and I would wait for as long as necessary to meet her on the ground.

CHAPTER TWENTY-SIX

JAKE SPARROW/ASHER CHRISTMAS

"Ash, is that you?" Gina called as soon as I set foot into the penthouse. By the hollow echo surrounding her voice, I could tell she was in the kitchen.

I found Gina sitting at the island, eating a grilled cheese sandwich. The smell of hot butter browning bread and melting cheese was a sign she had made it herself. She had also made herself at home in a pair of silk pajamas, the blousy kind. That was different. Gina had always liked showing off her skin and curves.

I'd seen that look in her eyes a million times before. She was begging for my sympathy. "Really, I'm so sorry, Ash. I've had time to think about what I did, and I don't know what came over me. When I saw that woman, I just …" She closed her eyes and massaged her temples.

I positioned myself on the other side of the island. "What are you doing here, Gina?"

She opened her eyes and set her hands in her lap. "A friend told me she saw you at a party last night. I thought if you were in town, then I might find you at the mansion or here. I tried here first, and that was when I ran into her." She scowled. "She's a doctor?"

My face felt tight, and I had a headache. "Now what?"

"What do you mean?"

"You found me. Now what?"

She sat her sandwich back on the plate. "I'm not telling your family where you are, if that's what you're worried about. You know I wouldn't do that to you. But haven't you heard?"

"Haven't I heard what?"

She studied me then sighed. "So much is happening in your world, Ash. And I'm telling you it's about to come crashing down. First …" She shoved an opened envelope at me. "I found this in my room, where your girlfriend was sleeping."

My neck jutted forward as I read who the letter was addressed to. "That belongs to Penina?"

She dropped it onto the counter. "Read it."

I pressed my finger on it. "You opened her mail?"

She snatched the envelope from under the tip of my finger. "You have to put yourself in my shoes, Ash. I walk into *my* place, and there's mail on the dresser for someone I don't know. What was I supposed to do?" she asked, throwing her hands up in a helpless manner.

"You suspected I was here, and if that was the case, then Penina was associated with me. That's why you should've checked with me before you infringed on her privacy."

"I knew you weren't going to read it, so I did. She's been coded, Ash."

I frowned. "What do you mean, 'she's been coded'?"

"Spence has made a deal with all the commercial DNA test centers in existence. If a person comes up as being an illegitimate child of Arthur Valentine or your father, they're coded."

My frown deepened as I processed what she was insinuating. Then I had to see what the hell she meant. I went against my better judgment and took the envelope from her then pulled out the paper.

"Look at the bottom," she said.

It had the name and number for the indemnity fund, headed by the Jada and Spencer Christmas

Foundation. It asked her to call the phone number below to unlock her DNA results and to speak with an agent to schedule an appointment with a local counselor regarding parentage. She was entitled to a healthy restitution for abuses against a primary relative of Randolph Wesley Christmas, Arthur G. Valentine, or both.

I grabbed a handful of my shirt over my heart and whispered, "What the fuck."

Gina sat watching me with concern, but she appeared to be a hundred miles away. I had to read the note at the bottom of the page again.

"Either she's your sister, or she's Valentine's daughter. Julia's sister," she added, whispering.

Fuck, Julia. She and I hadn't been involved since my father was alive. She was Valentine's daughter. Our relationship was not healthy and was merely transactional on her part. She was scared as hell of Jasper, but most people were. My oldest brother's reputation preceded him. Most saw him as a hard, bitter man who was unable to love, the sort of asshole who would rip his foes' heads off and feed the rest of their bodies to the vultures. Of course, his treachery was overexaggerated. Sure, his enemies had better watch out. But those whom Jasper loved, he loved unconditionally and dutifully. He hadn't loved Julia and guaranteed her he never would. If they had married, it would've been for business only. But just like nearly every woman who crossed my brother's path, she wanted him to want her for real.

Julia's ego was the size of the fucking galaxy. She'd seduced me because she thought it would make Jasper jealous. I would admit now what I couldn't then, that I returned her affections because I wanted a small taste of what Jasper had. But either he hadn't known about me and Julia, or he hadn't given a damn.

Jasper hadn't gotten jealous over a woman until the day Holly Henderson showed up for the annual Christmas with Christmases gathering seven years ago. I thought he would ask Holly Henderson to leave the estate once he learned who she was and why she was there. But he didn't. It was no surprise he married her. Julia was stupid, thinking she could manipulate Jasper into wanting her for real. But I was the bigger fool for getting entangled with her.

However, that wasn't why my blood felt as if it had turned into stone.

"Fuck," I whispered, thinking about all the ways in which I'd fucked Penina and the many more positions I had in store for us. I didn't want to stop doing her. I wanted her to be in my life forever but not as a fucking sibling. I had enough of those.

Gina shrugged. "Look on the bright side. Your family has already survived some serious inbreeding. I think that's why Randolph was so fucked up."

I narrowed my eyes at her. She was agitating the hell out of me, but she had a point. The Christmases were originally Mobleys. My great-great-grandparents Sylvester Mobley and Jane Young were raised as cousins, but the rumor was they were actually brother and sister. They'd fucked, she got pregnant, and to escape public scorn, they snuck off to America with a lot of family money and changed their surname to Christmas.

"That's a rumor," I said, even though I believed it to be true.

She rolled her eyes. "Oh, it's true, and you know it. But Penina"—Gina spoke her name with scorn —"being your sister isn't why I hate her. She's too fucking perfect. That's why I hate her. But ..." She took a bite of her sandwich. "But eating is helping me get over it. Want one?" She sounded like she had too much sandwich in her mouth.

"No, I don't want one." I slammed the letter from the DNA company onto the counter.

"So did you guys have sex?" she asked.

"Yes," I replied, too preoccupied to refine my answer.

Gina sat up straight, eyes wide. "Was she better than me?"

I scratched the back of my ear. I used to enjoy saying hurtful shit to her. I wanted to make her hurt for being in love with my other brother, Spencer, while involved with me. "You really want me to answer that question?"

She looked down and squirmed. "I was fucked up, wasn't I?"

"We both were," I said.

She looked up again. "Do you know I haven't had sex since the last time we tried?"

I jerked my head back. "Really?"

She shrugged. "I mean, I've had customers. Like ten of them, back to back, didn't want to fuck. Then I finally got one who did, and I just couldn't let him inside. We were in a hotel room in Toronto." She swallowed as a pained expression overtook her face. "He wasn't bad-looking, no halitosis, no furry body, but I just felt so fucking dirty. So ..." She shook her head. "Neglectful of myself."

I swallowed. "I'm proud of you."

She watched me with watery eyes. "Me too."

Gina knew I couldn't sleep. She didn't used to be able to either, but she yawned and told me that now she slept like a baby. We were sharing a bottle of rum. I tried to focus on what she was saying as she told me about the girls she worked with and how happy they had made her.

"But, Ash ..." Her eyes trailed from my face down to my dick. "You look so different. I hardly recognize you. You're so manly, Spencer-like."

"Ha," I scoffed, feeling relaxed even though I didn't want to be relaxed, not with Penina gone. "He's married, you know."

"I know," she snapped. "To another fucking Pollyanna like Jasper's wife. And look at you. You're sniffing after one who's a carbon copy of them. What about me?"

I watched her intently. Gina was a survivor, always had been and always would be. She was a young runaway and prostitute, used and abused by every man she'd ever encountered, even my father. We'd first crossed paths in the secret tunnels at the Christmas mansion. I was twelve, she was fourteen, and somebody had roughed her up. She was bleeding from her mouth, nose, and private parts. I was devastated and scared, but I knew I couldn't just leave her. I was too afraid to ask Jasper for help because he might have told Father. Even then, I knew who was responsible for her circumstances. So I asked if I could help clean her up, and she shouted at me to go to hell and leave her alone. I said no and held my ground. It wasn't like I'd found a wild cat or stray dog. She was a human being, a pretty little girl who wasn't much older than I was.

I had seen them before—girls my age shuffling through the dark tunnels, eyes to the ground, keeping a rapid pace. But I'd never run into one in Gina's condition.

"Go," she said, shooing me away while hugging her knees tighter.

"No!" I shouted, shaking my head. "I can't leave you here to die."

When I had said that, something seemed to click inside her. She asked me my name, and I told her. She laughed wildly and said that my father had done that to her.

"Then I hate him," I said, which wasn't hard to say because it was true.

"Me too," she replied.

We sat in silence, listening to cold, stale air pushing through the hallway.

"Okay," she finally said.

"Okay what?"

"I'll let you help me."

I went over to help her stand, and I learned why she had been sitting there in the first place. One of her legs was broken. She couldn't walk. I had to muster all my strength to carry her to my bedroom, which had an attached bathroom. I washed her, dried her, and let her sleep in my bed. Since she had the broken leg, I had to confide in Jasper. All he said was that he would handle it. Gina was taken out of my room and put into one of the guest rooms. A doctor and a nurse came to put her leg in a cast. I visited her as much as I could.

Then one evening, I asked her to join us for dinner at the main table. My parents rarely ate with their children. But it just so happened that on that night, Randolph showed up. He asked who Gina was.

"She's my friend."

He frowned indifferently and went on having a conversation with Jasper about needing him in the city to sit in on a meeting when he got out of school that day. He said the helicopter would pick him up at four, then he got up and walked out of the dining room without a second glance at the rest of us.

Later, when I asked Gina why he hadn't noticed her, she said that when my father was fucking and being an animal, a demon from within took over him. The man was buried somewhere inside, but the monster, the fiend, growled, gnashed his teeth, bit, punched, stomped, and didn't care what hole he put his dick in.

That was how I'd become her savior. Then she became my family. We tried being lovers, but she was too fucked up. Earlier, when I'd asked Gina to leave, she didn't comply because she knew if she stayed, I wouldn't make her go until she was ready to. As far as I was concerned, she was another sister. I loved her just as much as I did Bryn.

"You're not going to answer, are you?" she asked.

"What about you?" I asked, repeating her question.

She cleared her throat. "Yes." Her voice cracked regardless.

I was still lost for words. I could never love Gina in that way. Neither could Spencer. Although she never wanted to see it. As a wife, she would've been a constant reminder of our family's dark past. It wasn't her fault, though—that was how life worked sometimes.

"Once, I caught my father in the tunnels with a

girl—young, so damn young," I said, filling the silence between us. "I asked him what he was doing. He said she'd come to claim her mother's paycheck, and he was showing her out. Then he told me to get the fuck out of the tunnels, and they weren't built for me to play in. But I kept playing in them because I knew I'd run into another girl, and I did. You."

Gina tossed her head back and grunted bitterly. "Is that the memory I incite in you? I incite in all of you?" Her voice cracked. "I'm just a filthy little whore in the tunnels."

My jaw slackened. I couldn't believe she'd said that. "No." My tone was emphatic. "After all the fucking years you've been in my life, how could you say that?"

"You left me, Ash!" she shouted at the top of her lungs.

"I had to leave everybody, all of it," I yelled back. "Fuck. I had to take care of myself, Gina."

The silence was a welcomed ally at the moment.

I hadn't realized how heavily I was breathing until I said, "I cleaned you up. I let you sleep in my bed. I brought you food. We made you family. That's the ultimate kind of love."

Her chin trembled as the corners of her mouth pulled downward. "I know," she whispered then sniffed and swiped the tears off her cheeks with the backs of her hands. "I'm just afraid ..."

"What are you afraid of?" I asked as I got a cloth napkin out of the drawer and handed it to her.

She scrunched up her face and said, "I'm filthy and dirty and ..."

I shot a hand up. "Could you stop saying that? You're not filthy and dirty."

Gina pressed her lips together and wiped her face.

"Have you sought therapy?" I asked.

"No," she said and sniffed.

"Someone who has suffered the way you have has to. I know some very good ones."

She snorted. "You sound like a doctor."

I cracked a smile. "I *am* a doctor—a surgeon."

Finally, her face lit up. "I know. I'm very happy for you."

"And listen"—I leaned toward her to make sure she was looking me in the eye—"I'm a man. Therefore, I can say with certainty that we don't think that way—at least a mature guy doesn't. We don't give a fuck about who you were before we met you. We only care about who you are now."

She messed up her hair, which was something she did when she became anxious. "Ash, I'm glad you're okay. I'm going to leave in the morning. Thanks for the good advice. Also, I'm open to hearing your suggestions for a good therapist, and finally, I don't think you know."

I grimaced, confused. "Know what?"

"It's out there."

"What's out there?"

She cocked her head and raised an eyebrow. "What happened in Randolph's room before he died?"

I glared at her, refusing to say a word.

"It's in the news. Jasper's done a pretty good job of casting doubt and getting ahead of it, but the accusation is still out there. Lots of people believe that you and Bryn killed Randolph."

I closed my eyes and rubbed my forehead. I'd promised never to speak about it without Bryn's permission. And I was going to keep that promise.

"Thanks for letting me know," I said.

She nodded softly. "If you killed him, then good for you. He was a roach, a hard-to-kill parasite," she said, baring her teeth and curling her fingers as if she were choking his neck. Then her expression softened. "But anyway. Do you want to fuck or not?"

My expression was incredulous as I shook my head. "Hasn't anything I said resonated with you?"

She waggled her eyebrows. "I just remember how fat your dick was—pure fun. I figured since you're on a break, why not?"

"I'm not on a break."

"You better let her know that. She's hot, sexy. I'm sure some guy is trying to fuck her as we're speaking." She slapped herself on the chest. "Hell, I want to fuck her."

I felt for my keys in my pocket as I stood. "We're not fucking, Gina." There was no need to mention that sex was never good between us.

She flopped a hand dismissively. "Whatever. I'm going to bed. I'm flying back to Colorado in the morning." She walked seductively to the wall that separated the living room from the hallway. Gina grabbed on to the plaster and arched her back while sticking out her chest. "Maybe I'll see you later tonight."

Then she was out of sight.

I shook my head. I wasn't going to sleep in the same house with her. I was accustomed to her tricks. She would slip into the bed with me in the middle of the night. I wouldn't be asleep, but she would do whatever she could to get me to stick it into her. It was odd because she'd informed me on several occasions that she never felt a thing when a man stuck his dick in. Spencer was the only exception to that, not me.

The knowledge that she preferred him over me used to make me insane and send me on a downward spiral of doing whatever it took to steal her attention from him. Shit, that felt as if it all had occurred a lifetime ago. She and Spencer could race off into the sunset and live happily ever after in hell if they wanted. The decision was theirs. I loved and craved Penina Ross. The night's interaction with Gina only confirmed it further.

I WALKED TO THE HOSPITAL, NEEDING THE WARM night air and exercise to help me get to sleep. I was going on thirty-six hours without it. My hands were jittery, and my mind was filled with thoughts that would interfere with me effectively using a scalpel. I needed to sleep for at least four hours.

When I made it to the front of the medical complex, I stopped to behold my brand-new purchase. Fuck, I couldn't believe I had done it. What was more surprising was that Jasper hadn't traced the purchase to me. I'd used the alias Pete Sykes to buy it. Jasper had set up the account when our father was alive. Spencer, Bryn, and I were able to draw uncapped funds from it at will without our father finding out what we were doing with the money. Jasper was the one who hid our purchases. Up until his last breath, it never sank into Randolph's head that his oldest son was his greatest invention and fiercest adversary. It was as if defying our father gave Jasper a hard-on.

I stuffed my hands deeper into my pants pockets and leaned my head back to get a look at the top of the structure. Maybe I wanted Jasper to find me. I missed him like a son did his father.

Five and a half years ago, after his wife's tell-all on our family was released, I started playing with the idea of changing everything about myself—new name, identity, personality. Everything about me would be different. First, I dyed my hair darker. Then I shredded my driver's license and passport. Next, I drained all the cash out of Asher Christmas's bank account and converted it to cryptocurrency. Then one morning, after a short sleep, I woke up and said my name was Jake Sparrow. I knew a guy named Grey Lansing, who had been a rich drifter, but nowadays he spent most his time in San Francisco. Grey was able to get me full-on identification as Jake Sparrow, which included a driver's license, a birth certificate, social security cards, and school records. Grey warned me that I had to know my limitations, though. If I was going to put Asher Christmas to rest, then I would have to make sure I didn't end up in a situation where I was being taken downtown by the cops and fingerprinted. That was the only scenario in which he couldn't make Asher and Jake match. Staying out of legal trouble was easy. I was too smart to get arrested for anything—not that I would get away with murder, but crime was never my thing, which was why I was insulted that Gina would question whether I would murder Randolph. I hadn't, but someone had. And I knew who it was.

"Good night, Dr. Sparrow," someone said.

I brought my gaze down. It was a nurse. "Good night Lane," I replied.

The cordialities between us put a smile on my face. It was the hospital that had ultimately saved me—getting to know nurses and doctors. You had to have a fucking heart of gold to do what we did, period. I'd bought the business because I knew the power of what it did for people. It was an easy decision for Jake Sparrow. As far as Asher Christmas, I had put him in a box and stored him away. He would never have considered buying a hospital, and he wouldn't have said good night to Lane. I'd learned to cut Asher a break, though. He came off as an entitled prick, but he wasn't. He had no fucking self-love. But one look at Gina, and Asher sprang back to life. Like Rip Van Winkle waking up after a long sleep, finding out the world was different—that was happening to the part of me that was Asher Christmas. I was still thinking about that when I headed inside.

I WALKED INTO MY OFFICE, KEEPING THE LIGHTS OFF, then dropped onto the sofa, kicked off my shoes, and lay back to stare at the ceiling. I would've called Penina, but I'd gotten her message loud and clear—she didn't want to talk to me. I chose to listen to Zara's advice and leave her be. When Penina was ready to say something to me, I would know.

"Damn it." I sat up straight. She and I could be closely related. I couldn't wait until she called the number to get the results. I needed to know sooner rather than later. *Is she a Valentine or a Christmas?*

I needed a biological sample from Penina to be tested. The mask she'd worn the previous night hadn't covered her mouth, so it was likely her saliva wouldn't be on it. Plus, Kirk had taken the mask back to the mansion and locked it in the case with the others. The concierge had picked up the box that contained her attire. The maids had also cleaned, and they had done a thorough job.

I turned to think and caught sight of my desk. We'd fucked earlier and made out like crazy. I hadn't washed my face, so I had Penina's saliva all over me. I took my phone out of my pocket, called Si, and asked if he could do me a favor.

"Dr. Sparrow," said a woman.

I sat up quickly and caught a glimpse of Melanie the OR assistant before I rubbed my eyes. "Shit, what time is it?"

We both turned to the clock on my table. It was eight a.m. The previous night had been crazy. I'd swiped my face for DNA samples from Penina, then I swabbed the inside of my mouth. Si came in and turned the samples in to the lab, advising them to put a rush on it. I thanked him.

"I'm not even going to ask what that was about," he said before going home and back to bed.

Knowing that the samples were being processed relaxed me. The next time I lay down on the sofa in my office, I'd closed my eyes and thought of nothing, hoping that would help me sleep. It had.

"You're due in surgery. We've been waiting for you for the past hour. Deb just suggested we check your office."

I shook the cobwebs out of my head. *An hour ago?* The surgery was supposed to start at seven a.m.

"We're just not used to you being in here. No one thought to check in here until now," she added.

I held up a hand to let her know I wasn't upset. "It's okay, Melanie." I sighed deeply as I stood. "Okay. Here I come. Tell everyone I apologize for keeping them waiting."

"It's okay, Dr. Sparrow." She cracked a small smile. "We all knew you needed the sleep. You're the hardest-working man in the hospital."

I snorted a chuckle as I pointed at her. "And don't you forget it."

Melanie laughed on her way out.

Damn, I liked my surgical teams at the hospital. I wondered if they would return the same sentiment if they ever found out I'd been lying to them about who I was.

CHAPTER TWENTY-SEVEN

PENINA ROSS

"Who's that?" Aunt Christine asked.

We were in the rental car on our way to the coroner's office. I had scrolled through all of Jake's text messages. I was on my third read of each one, forgetting that I should probably focus on who I was in the car with.

"A guy," I said. "A surgeon—an attending, actually."

"Then you're not involved romantically with him?"

I looked at her with my mouth agape. I truly didn't know the answer to that question. He had said in several of his text messages that Gina was not his girlfriend. He also said that Gina was threatened by me and had admitted to overstating the nature of her relationship with him. It almost sounded as if he was making excuses for her.

"I don't know anymore," I replied.

"Why don't you know?"

I stiffened. I was surprised she had asked me that question. Christine had never seemed that interested in my love life.

"I don't know why I don't know," I finally said.

She stole a glance at me. "You know I'm a therapist, right?"

I smiled faintly. "Are you offering me a free session?"

She turned on the blinker and checked her driver's side mirror. "Sure, let's give it a go. So, tell me anything you want about this guy who's made you confused."

I wondered how honest I should be. It felt odd engaging in the sort of conversation she was inviting me to have with her. I'd really never let Christine see behind my curtain. However, the other night, we'd made some leeway, a breakthrough. We were closer. And with my mother's death, she and I were all that was left of the Rosses.

"There's a doctor," I said then sighed as I massaged my temples.

"Okay, we've established that. What do you want to tell me about this doctor?" she asked.

"I think I love him," I said.

"You think you love him?"

I recounted the first time Jake and I had made real eye contact and how later I discovered he was not only a surgeon at the hospital but also my attending.

"I mean, is fate a real thing?" I asked.

"Absolutely." Her voice rang with real optimism.

I was glad to hear it. Then I told her about the night of the fire and his fancy, full-service penthouse. I mentioned how he'd left me flowers every morning along with a continental breakfast spread fit for the Ritz.

"So he's wealthy beyond what the job pays?" she asked.

"Exactly," I said and continued recounting my short but impactful relationship with a man whose real name I'd just recently learned.

Christine turned into the parking lot just as I was revisiting what had happened at the masquerade party when the masked woman approached us and asked if he was someone she knew.

"And was he?" she asked.

"I think he was."

"Then you believe he wasn't being honest with you in regard to the woman at the party?"

I thought hard about all the circumstances that started and ended the degradation of what was shaping up to be the greatest night of my life.

"Well ..." I pressed my lips together harder, wondering if I should reveal Jake's—or Asher's—secret. "Am I on the clock?"

"On the clock?"

"Yes, do I have doctor-patient privileges here?"

She nodded graciously. "Do you have a dollar on you?"

I opened my purse then my wallet. I only had six twenties and a ten. I took out the ten. "I have ten dollars."

Christine smiled as she rubbed her hands together. "I'll use it to buy us expensive handcrafted coffees with loads of sugar, fat, and caffeine. So, let's hear it."

I laughed. Up until then, I'd never known my aunt had the slightest hint of a sense of humor. It was almost tragic that it had taken such a sad occasion for me to learn that.

I focused on the red brick building. Going

against every instinct in my body that knew secrets were supposed to be stored deep inside the brain and padlocked, I said, "I know the woman at the party recognized him because yesterday I was told by a woman claiming to be his girlfriend that his name is Asher Christmas."

Christine jolted herself out of her relaxed position and looked at me with bulging eyes. "His name is what?"

Time seemed to slow down as I said, "Asher Christmas."

A bitter laugh escaped her then started to build into a more hearty but strange one. "This fucking world never ceases to amaze me."

"I don't understand," I said, my voice barely audible. My face was warm, and my heart was beating a mile a minute.

Christine put a hand on her chest and took a deep breath. "I'm sorry, Pen. I just ..." She closed her eyes and shook her head. When she looked at me again, she appeared more focused. "We have to get through this next part of our day. After that, we must talk about Asher Christmas. Are you okay with that?"

I didn't know if I could wait. I swallowed repeatedly, thinking about the right way to handle all the anxiety I was feeling. Then my gaze fell on the building again. Mary Ross was inside, lying on a slab. Asher or Jake was a man I just met. The least I could do was focus solely on her before her body was committed to the ground.

Decision made, I swallowed again to relieve the tightness in my throat. "I'm fine with it." It came out clear but jittery from the intense pain in my heart.

CHRISTINE AND I DIDN'T NEED TO SIT AND WAIT. THE clerk who greeted us was a slight woman who appeared to be in her mid-to-late forties. She shifted a thick brown folder she was carrying from her right to her left hand to shake. The woman referred to my aunt as Dr. Ross, then she said her name was Scheana. Then she shook my hand. I told her my name was Penina.

"She's a neurosurgeon in New Orleans," my aunt added.

Scheana lifted her eyebrows. "Then I'm in the company of two Dr. Rosses."

I felt my face flush as Christine smiled proudly. It

was the first time my professional stature had been confirmed in front of my aunt, and it made me feel bashful but delighted. Scheana announced there had been new developments in the case and that we should follow her somewhere so we could speak in private.

Christine and I looked at each other with furrowed brows then followed Scheana through a doorway. My head felt as if it were detached from my body as we walked down a carpeted hallway with no windows or doors. Scheana asked Christine if it had been difficult to find the medical examiner's office, and my aunt answered that it hadn't been since she had been there before. Christine shared that she had been there in February of that year to identify the body of one of her clients. I kept my arms folded, nostrils flared, wondering why I couldn't smell the slightest scent of dead bodies. It was as if corpses weren't in the building, or we were being escorted far away from the morgue.

"Oh yeah," Scheana said as she led us around another corner.

"Yes, Detective Knight called and asked if I could identify the body in person."

"And you came all the way from Boston?"

"Absolutely," Christine said as Scheana opened

the door for us. "So, I know we're nowhere near following normal protocols for identifying a body."

"That's correct," Scheana said once we were all in the small room, which had a table with two chairs on each side of it and a whiteboard that had nothing written on it. She pointed at two of the chairs. "Please, have a seat."

Since the small talk was over, my anxiety was back in spades. Christine must've noticed, because she held my hand under the table.

Scheana took the seat across from us, setting the folder she was carrying on top of the table. Her smile was tight but genial—it was the sort that said she was about to apologize for something. "We received a corrected report on the deceased's fingerprints this morning. We're very sorry for alarming you, but …"

Christine slapped one hand on her chest and squeezed my shoulder with the other. "The deceased is not Mary."

"No," Scheana said in a humble tone. "We've identified her as Laurel Hempstead from Portland, Maine."

"But this woman had my sister's identification and my grandmother's locket?"

Scheana nodded softly and said, "Yes. She also

had a criminal record a mile long. Mostly identity fraud, but the personal item that belonged to your sister, which the deceased had possession of, says that at some point, the two may have come in contact." Then she took a large brown envelope out of the thick folder and emptied the contents, which included the locket and my mother's social security card and driver's license, onto the table.

I fixed my gaze on the picture of the woman on the license. I couldn't clearly remember my mother's face, but I knew one thing for sure. "The woman in that photograph is not my mother."

Scheana folded her hands on the table. "We are now aware of that." Once again, she sounded remorseful.

I hadn't noticed until then that Christine had opened the locket and was handling it like it was precious.

My aunt's chin quivered as she looked at me. "It belongs to your grandmother." Her voice was strained.

I leaned back, blinking rapidly, wondering if I'd heard her correctly. "You mean 'belonged.'"

Her eyes were watery. "Belongs."

"They're alive?"

"Remember what I explained to you about them

last night? Your mother and I are dead to them, but as far as living and breathing, yes, they're alive."

SILENCE LOOMED, SETTLING IN THE AIR WITH THE density and murkiness of a swamp creature. Christine and I were back in the car. Obviously, we had a lot to talk about.

Finally, she fell back against the driver's seat and heaved a sigh. "Where do you want to start?"

Since I learned my grandparents were alive, I'd actually been doing a lot of thinking about that question. Although I was curious about them and oddly ashamed of how they'd treated their daughters, I'd never had an emotional tie to them.

"We have to find my mother," I said.

"I know," she replied then rotated her body to face me. "But I think it's time I tell you what I know about the Christmases."

I felt my chest cave in as I nodded.

"I'm sure you've figured out that the money I send you each month doesn't come from my parents' trust."

I hadn't thought about that until she mentioned it. "It makes sense," I said.

She had to brace herself again. "So …" she began at the bottom of another breath. "Your mother was held against her will and sexually violated, repeatedly and in unimaginable ways. You can't imagine how severe abuse changes a human being forever. And truly, only the very strong can survive it."

I closed my eyes and pressed my lips together, trying to keep myself from crying. All I could picture was my mom as a little girl being hurt in such a horrible manner. I wanted to use my scalpel to operate on her past and remove the cancer of her experience.

Christine was a blur through my tear-filled eyes. "Is she very strong?"

Her pressed lips answered the question for me. She hadn't considered my mother durable enough to cope with her past.

"Sweetheart," Christine said in a gentle tone.

Unstoppable waterworks streamed down my face, but I was able to open my eyes enough to take the tissues Christine handed to me. I wiped the tears out of my eyes, blew my nose enough to clear my sinuses, and braced myself to hear more.

"Are you ready to continue?" she asked.

Unable to speak, I nodded.

"Your father could be one of two men—Arthur Valentine or Randolph Christmas."

My eyes grew so wide that I thought they would pop out. "What?"

"I'm sorry, Pen. We should find out which of those men fathered you."

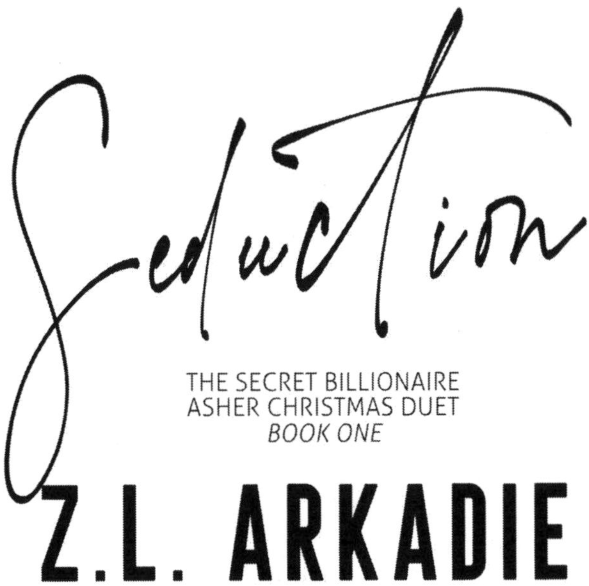

THE SECRET BILLIONAIRE
ASHER CHRISTMAS DUET
BOOK ONE

Z.L. ARKADIE

ISBN: 978-1-952101-09-0

❀ Created with Vellum